PETE'S DRAGON

PETE'S DRAGON

Adapted from Walt Disney Productions'
screen presentation by

Dewy Moffatt

NEW ENGLISH LIBRARY/TIMES MIRROR

First NEL paperback edition October 1978

NEL Books are published by
New English Library Limited
from Barnard's Inn, Holborn,
London EC1N 2JR
Made and printed in Great Britain by
Hazell Watson & Viney Ltd,
Aylesbury, Bucks

45003837 8

Chapter One

Dusk had fallen and in the New England woods the sultry air was stifling. Jagged lightning pierced the darkening sky; thunder rumbled, the sound ominous and full of menace. Lightning flashed again, briefly illuminating gnarled trees, tangled roots, and a jungle of bracken and fern. The glow had a more startling sight to reveal: a young boy moving rapidly through the air as though astride a huge animal. The branches parted mysteriously as he passed through. Every now and again he peered nervously over his shoulder, his eyes strained and anxious.

When he almost collided with a sturdy branch he swiftly ducked his head, calling softly, 'Elliott, put me down.'

At once the boy stopped moving, and for a moment he was poised motionless in mid-air. Then with a lithe movement he swung one leg over and slid to the ground. He stood irresolute, blinking in the darkness. Pete, aged nine, was a good-looking boy with a shock of red hair, clear blue eyes and a light, freckled skin. But now, dirt streaked one cheek and he looked tousled, his faded blue denims grubby and torn.

Footsteps crashed through the dense undergrowth, the sharp, angry buzz of voices clearly audible. A look of panic crossed Pete's face. His escape from the treacherous Gogan family had not gone unnoticed. He had hardly expected it would.

It was at the turn of the century, a time when orphans could be sold for a fifty dollar fee. Unfortunately, they sometimes fell into the hands of unscrupulous foster parents. Pete had met with just such a fate. From the day the Gogans first took him from the orphanage he had received ruthless treatment. Used solely as a slave he had been bullied, beaten and forced to do heavy chores until weariness made him drop.

Now in a desperate bid for freedom he needed a place to lie low. If they caught him . . . he shuddered, knowing a moment of sheer terror.

There wasn't a second to lose. Examining the heavy undergrowth he saw a deep hollow at the base of a tree.

'They're getting close,' he whispered to an invisible companion. 'We'd better hide here.'

He darted towards the cavity but the next moment was flung forward, almost falling. Reproachfully, he stared upward. 'Stop swinging your tail,' he murmured. 'You almost knocked me down.'

A strange musical sound, pleasing, not quite human, reassured him. Pete repressed a tiny smile and parted the underbrush. A large, invisible body climbed into the space and settled down with a soft snort. Pete followed, concealing himself at the base of the tree.

Crouching low, he breathed, 'Here they come. Squish down.'

Clumsy footsteps lumbered closer and Pete's face screwed into a mask of fear. Soaked, shivering, he raked glistening wet leaves around him in a further effort to remain hidden. In his present plight he wished that he, too, had the ability to make himself invisible.

Seconds later the four members of the Gogan family emerged from a clump of trees. Mr Gogan carried a lantern and in its flickering light they presented a fearsome spectacle. Their faces were evil, their hair matted and filthy, their clothing ragged. Naturally lazy, unused to trekking they stumbled through the dense bush wielding cumbersome clubs and bickering at every step.

Petrified, Pete held his breath aware that the slightest movement would betray him. In the rapidly fading light the group squinted at the ground, eagerly searching for tell-tale signs of the runaway.

Grover, an uncouth lout in his twenties indicated the way ahead. 'He's gone that way.'

'He went this way,' contradicted his brother Willie. 'He's up a tree, I think!'

Merle Gogan signalled angrily to his sons to make less noise. His mean face was hard as granite. He didn't want Pete warned of their approach. Just wait until he caught up with him. Lena Gogan stumbled into a clearing and probed at surrounding bushes with her club. Merle glared at his wife. Noted for an explosive temper at the best of times, he was in a perfectly foul mood. Lena should have watched the boy – not let him out of her sight. He sucked the holes in his yellow teeth and spat.

Lena had no wish to further incur her husband's wrath. A pool of pale yellow light cast by the lantern showed her to be an awesome sight. She was dumpy with grey, stringy hair, small fierce eyes buried in pouches of fat, and a muddy complexion. Her lips fell back in a snarl, revealing a missing front tooth.

In a vain attempt to sound kindly, she called, 'Oh, Pee-eete . . .! Peee-eeete . . .! Where are you? Please come ba-ack! You're like a real son to us! We miss-s-s you!'

Pete quivered, icy cold with fear.

Lena's voice dropped to a rasping, ugly whisper. 'If I get near 'im, you can bet I won't miss 'im with this!' In one vicious

movement she swung her hefty club whacking a patch of ferns to the ground.

Grover and Willie watched, attempting to smother their coarse laughter but they could not keep their guffaws in check. Ignorant, lumbering young men in their twenties, they fell over each other, holding their stomachs.

Their mother glowered, silencing them. They did not care to be on the receiving end of one of her well-aimed blows. Composing her ugly face into the semblance of a smile she cupped her bony fingers to her mouth and sang:

> 'I'll cook you cake and gingerbread,
> Bring you tea in bed, on a tray.'

Merle's cracked voice took up the next lines . . .

> 'We'll slave while you go fishin';
> You'll get permission to run and play.'

Lena pretended to weep . . .

> 'These tears oughta show you I care.
> Come back; by cracky we'll share
> The happiest home in these hills.'

But the Gogan brothers made no attempt to disguise their true feelings towards Pete:

> 'Gonna snag him, gag him, drag him through town;
> Put his head in the river, let the pup drown;
> Trap him, strap him, wrap him in a sack – yeah!
> Tie him screamin' to a railroad track.'

Merle Gogan took a softer line:

> 'We'll have you sing in chapel;
> You'll be the apple of Mama's eye.'

Lena backed him up . . .

> 'I'll tend to all your sewin',
> And do the mowin',
> So jes' rely on me.
> Dang, we know you're out there.
> It's late – we're waitin' to share

The happiest home in these hills,
In these hills.'

The unkind brothers took up their chant . . .

'Gonna paw him, claw him, saw him in half;
When he cries for mercy, we'll just laugh;
Beat him, heat him, eat him for dessert – yeah!'

Lena sneered and said softly,

'Roast him gently so the flames won't hurt!'

Grover and Willie guffawed, pummelling each other. Frustrated and furious, Lena pulled them apart. 'Now, spread out and find him,' she shrieked.

Sulkily, the two boys picked themselves off the ground and sloped off into the woods, swinging their clubs as they went.

Still optimistic, Lena continued to sing in her rasping voice:

'You'll swim and you'll go campin';
You'll be a champion in your own backyard.
Our love is overflowin', it keeps on growin';
We'll sleep good knowin' you're home!'

Pete, huddled in his hideaway was not fooled by Lena's sugary words. She was venomous as a snake. He sucked in his breath as the two brothers drew close.

Pete's invisible friend had been listening to the hypocrisy of the Gogan family and decided to take revenge . . . and a bit of fun. Willie walked past the underbrush and suddenly his legs were knocked from under him. He fell heavily, and face down, into thick, grey mud.

Pete's eyes widened. 'I told you not to swing your tail,' he warned his friend.

Willie lifted his head from the mud and stared up at his brother. 'Somethin' . . . hit me . . .' he gasped.

'What somethin'?' snapped Grover irritably.

Willie shook himself, sending mud in all directions. 'If I knowed what somethin', I wouldn't call it somethin', I'd call it by it's name.' He staggered to his feet.

Grover was unsympathetic. He shrugged and moved ahead.

But Elliott was not yet through with his tricks; in fact, as far as he was concerned the game was just starting.

Pete guessed his pal's intentions. 'No . . . no . . . don't . . .' he whispered urgently, but Elliott wasn't listening. Grover, too, was knocked violently to the ground and landed in a muddy pool. Willie found the incident amusing and laughed hysterically.

Grover spluttered, spat out a mouthful of mud and rounded on his brother, his face venomous. 'You tripped me . . .' he accused.

Willie shook his shaggy head. 'That wasn't a trip. That was done to you like it was done to me.'

'And you dunnit!' Grover swung his club at his brother.

'It wasn't me, I'm tellin' you!' protested Willie, trying to leap clear.

Grover was in no mood to listen. Convinced his brother was lying he struck him and seconds later the two of them were kicking, screaming and fighting like a pair of alley-cats.

Merle and Lena stumbled along the slippery path and Merle grabbed the boys, pulling them apart. He shook them viciously. 'Dumb polecats . . . fightin' it out while that little snake of a kid gits further away!'

'Why don' we jes' git ourselfs another orphan?' Willie's face was sullen, his voice churlish.

' 'Cause I paid our last fifty dollars for Pete, plus fifty cents legal fees,' cut in Lena sourly. 'I ain't got fifty more, plus legals . . . that's why!'

'It's the principle of the thing,' ranted Merle Gogan. He turned savagely towards his loutish sons. 'You understand about principles?'

Dumbly they shook their heads.

'Here's somethin' you'll understand,' spat their mother. 'We're all gonna hafta start workin' the farm with our own hands . . . unless you spot the little twerp!'

Grover and Willie exchanged shocked glances. The thought of toiling every day on the farm was too much for them. Pete must be found!

Lena peered into the gloom, her face crafty. The boy could not be far away . . . he hadn't had much of a start.

> 'Did you have to go strayin'?
> Please don't leave the farm!
> Can't you hear us prayin'
> That you'll be safe from harm?
> God bless you!'

Such deviousness was too much for Elliott. He swished his invisible tail. Wham! Into the mud went Lena, then Merle. Pete froze in fear and dug his finger nails into the palms of his hands. The Gogans were close . . . so perilously close.

The family splashed helplessly in the mud, their eyes rolling with fear as they tried to get to their feet. Spitting out brackish water they scraped their plastered hair from their faces.

Willie and Grover supported themselves against a tree trunk, muttering:

> 'We're gonna string him from a tree,
> We're gonna sting him like a bee,
> We're gonna spill him on his head,
> We're gonna fill him full of lead,
> In these hills!'

Merle and Lena slithered to a standing position. They were soaked and hungry, the woods were black and if they were going to find the runaway it wasn't going to be tonight. There was something very strange going on and they suddenly felt like abandoning the search. Muttering curses they stampeded back the way they had come. As she ran, Lena comforted herself with the thought that there would be another day. She was determined that the scallywag would not escape her clutches. He was fifty dollars-worth of investment which she did not intend to lose. She spat out a small pebble and lurched along the narrow path.

Their footsteps receded and Pete breathed a deep sigh of relief. Stiff and cold he emerged from the tree hollow and stretched. The thunder storm was almost over; only an occasional rumble vibrated in the distant hills.

He stared at the parted underbrush where his friend was sitting. 'We better stay right here,' Pete murmured. 'I'm tired. Aren't you?'

A soft, musical acknowledgement gave him the answer. Smiling, Pete crept into the foliage and snuggled close to the invisible Elliott. He closed his eyes and fatigue swept over him enveloping him in a heavy blanket. Within minutes he was asleep.

Chapter Two

Bars of golden sunlight penetrated the tangled foliage of the trees and shone warmly on Pete as he lay sleeping. He stirred, opening his eyes. For a fraction of a second he looked uncertain, then memory flooded back. He sat up and looked cautiously about. Were the dreaded Gogans nearby? No sound came to his ears other than the chorusing of birds in the sunlit glade. Yawning, he stood up. His muscles ached from lying in a hollow of wet leaves but at least he was safe. The fresh smell of dawn, the mingling scents of damp leaves and wet fields, the rapidly increasing light gave him a feeling of reassurance. Today was new, the air was warm. He felt a sudden glow of happiness.

Elliott was not lying in the dense undergrowth so Pete decided to look for him. He wandered along the woodland path watching the fluctuation of the sunlight on the high canopy of leaves. The trees thinned and as he came to a clearing he heard a steady munching sound.

'Hey, Elliott,' cried Pete. 'Whatcha doing?'

Elliott poked his head from the branches of an apple tree and smiled down at Pete. This morning he had materialised. He was a splendid dragon standing twelve feet tall, a vivid bright green all over except for a thatch of rose-pink hair and a splash of pink fringing at the tip of his tail. His compact, powerful wings were dove grey and altogether he was rather magnificent. Right now his good-humoured face looked rather funny as his cheeks bulged with apples.

Pete suddenly realised that he was hungry, too. 'I'm starved,' he announced.

Elliott tossed him down an apple and Pete sunk his teeth into the crisp, juicy fruit. Elliott continued to pluck a pile of apples from the tree and then sat down. Pete walked up the dragon's tail and sat comfortably on his large, round back.

'You sure changed my life! I didn't think I'd ever be happy till I met you,' Pete told his friend.

Elliott responded with a soft, half-human joyous sound and Pete tossed him another apple. Very soon there was only one left. Pete looked at it with longing but he decided to let Elliott have it. He was so big . . . it took a lot of food to fill up a dragon. 'You can have it, Elliott,' he said generously.

Elliott refused but just as Pete reached for the fruit, the dragon snatched it off the grass, tossing it into the air. Pete showed disappointment. Elliott belched a stream of bright, hot flame and moments later, Pete was enjoying a baked apple to round off his meal.

'Ummm . . . you're a good cook, Elliott,' said Pete, trying not to burn his fingers.

Elliott lowered his head and gave Pete a wet, sloppy kiss. Pete wiped his face. 'Behave yourself, Elliott,' he said with a wide, friendly grin. He skipped across the grass, pausing for a moment to gaze at the blue sky and the curve of sweeping hills which ran down to the sea. Elliott followed with an easy, rambling gait and after a while they played a game of tag. The fears of last night were behind them and Pete turned affectionately to Elliott and started to sing:

> 'I look in your eyes and you whisper sweetly.
> We don't match in size but we fit so neatly.
> It's nice waking up when you're close beside me,
> Humming in my ear . . .'

'Bop . . . bop . . . bop . . . bop . . .' replied Elliott.
Pete chorused happily,

> 'I love you, too.
> Remember the night when you first confided,
> And things went so right that we both decided;
> Now we're together and life is so perfect,
> Don't ever disappear . . .'

Elliott replied musically.

'Oh, really,' grinned Pete. 'Elliott, you're just saying that. But is it really true?'

The dragon nodded, his expressive eyes sentimental.

Pete danced a few steps on the lush grass, singing:

> 'I love you, too.
> We're walking down a road of our own,
> Where rain can never fall.
> I'm glad I don't have to be alone –
> You know what to say when I want direction;
> You don't turn away when I want protection;
> Your voice is the sound of an angel singing
> Music I wait to hear!'

'Bop . . . bop . . . bop . . .' chanted Elliott and in his near-human voice uttered, 'I love you!'

Pete tickled him. 'And I love you, too!'

Laughing, contented, they trudged over a hill towards a weather-beaten sign. Pete pointed to the long, strange word carved deep into the wood. 'Pas-sa-ma-quod-dy . . .' He spelled it aloud. 'Passamaquoddy. Mmmm . . . sounds like a nice place.'

Elliott made a sour grunt. He was perfectly happy in the hills. Why go to a village with a strange name?

Pete had already decided. He was going. 'Now, Elliott,' he said, 'we want the people of Passamaquoddy to like us, don't we?' His eyes pleaded for agreement.

Elliott heaved his broad green shoulders. He knew what Pete was going to request. He would ask him to disappear – yet stay close. This morning, Elliott was rather enjoying being visible . . . it was a pleasure he seldom allowed himself. People fussed so when they saw him.

Pete cocked his head to one side, surveying his friend. 'I mean, you're kinda big, and we don't want to scare anyone, do we?'

Elliott's giggle was mischievous. He was in the mood for fun. Perhaps he could surprise some unsuspecting person.

Pete sensed what was going on in the dragon's mind. 'So you better not show yourself to anyone . . . understand?'

Elliott protested . . . Pete was unrelenting. 'I know how you feel, but you'll *have* to make yourself invisible,' he insisted.

Elliott shook his frame and huge tears formed in his eyes. Life had too many frustrations. He didn't wish to upset Pete . . . and yet . . . He hit upon an idea. He wriggled and the bottom half of him vanished. He looked at Pete, hoping for approval.

Pete shook his head. 'I'm sorry . . . but the whole thing has to go.'

Elliott swallowed his disappointment, and gave in with a gentle sigh. Satisfied, Pete nodded and started down the winding dirt road towards the picturesque fishing village. As he plodded through a blanket of pine needles, Elliott poked him sharply in the back. The dragon felt forlorn and cheated. A tiny smile curved Pete's mouth upward but he ignored the push. When Elliott prodded him a second time, Pete turned and wagged a warning finger in the direction of the dragon's face. Elliott gave an invisible shrug and trotted meekly in Pete's tracks.

As Pete drew closer to the village he was entranced by the tiny community and its superb setting. Sturdy wooden houses painted in fresh pastel shades of pink, white, blue and yellow were surrounded by neat gardens with white picket fences. A tall church steeple graced the skyline and there was a ship's chandlery, a

16

tavern and dozens of fishing boats bobbing about in the harbour. The air was filled with the roar of angry surf surging shorewards, hurling spray over grey, jagged rocks. The smooth sandy beach stretched away as far as the eye could see. On a jutting point of land a tall, white lighthouse stood like a sentinel. Dazzling sunlight sparkled on the restless water and large birds glided low, tilting, swaying, shearing the waves with their wings. The tang of salty air blended subtly with the scent of the pine woods.

Pete inhaled deeply, enjoying his new-found freedom. Drawing closer to the village his footsteps began to drag. What sort of reception could he expect from a community of strangers? He could see the inhabitants clearly now, women in long skirts and bonnets, and men for the most part wearing fishermen's jerseys and peaked caps. When Pete and his unseen companion reached level ground, Pete comforted himself that no-one was likely to pay much attention to a small, ragged and rather grubby boy.

It was unfortunate that as Pete entered the village street, a ginger cat basking quietly on a patch of grass and enjoying the sun's warmth should suddenly raise its head. Elliott might be invisible to human beings but the cat was not so easily fooled. An expression of fear and confusion crossed its furry face. Jumping up, it arched its back, spitting in terror, its fur standing on end.

Pete whispered a swift warning. 'Elliott, stay close to me. And please . . . behave yourself!'

An egg delivery man clutching several crates of eggs frowned in surprise. Who was the kid talking to, he wondered. He dismissed Pete from his mind when he saw a likely customer. 'Get 'em by the dozen,' he advised.

The ginger cat still had its green orbs riveted upon Pete's unseen companion. Emitting a blood-curdling yowl of terror it raced between the eggman's legs. He cursed, the crates of eggs swayed precariously and he shouted, 'Whoops!' He noticed Pete nearby and had a hunch that he was at the root of the trouble. Muttering, 'Get 'em by the dozen,' he hurried up a garden path.

Pete continued along the High Street, picking up a stick as he walked. He drew it along the rails of a white picket fence. *Clack-clack-clack.* A man at the front door of the house was collecting his newspaper, and looked round sharply. His look of disapproval turned to one of sheer astonishment. Each picket of the fence had snapped clean in half. But how? Pete, blissfully unaware that Elliott was swishing his powerful tail and snapping the pickets like matchsticks, ambled nonchalantly along the street.

He drew level with the milkman's horse. By nature a docile creature she pricked up her ears, glanced nervously over her shoulder, then whinnied in fear. She reared up, pawing the air.

The milkman, shocked at the animal's unexpected behaviour, fell over his crate and smashed all the bottles. The milk formed a creamy pool in the gutter. The milkman glared and his eyes lit on Pete. He pointed an accusing finger. 'You scared my horse,' he yelled.

Pete backed away, shaking his head. 'It wasn't me . . . it was . . .' His sentence froze into silence. How could he say it was his dragon who was upsetting all the animals in the town? Pete did the only thing he could think of at that moment. He took to his heels.

Chaos was to follow!

As the horse galloped away, and the eggman leapt to safety, the town's cement man was completing the very first pavement. As he worked he looked up occasionally to read with pride a notice saying 'FIRST CEMENT SIDEWALK IN MAINE'. Lovingly, he smoothed over the last few inches. Once the pavement had dried, he intended to be the very first person to walk on it. An uproar at his back and the sound of running feet made him look round. His smile of pride froze on his face. Protectively he raised his hand as the eggman, the milkman and a horse all thundered towards his precious cement pavement.

'Stay away! Stay away!' he bellowed waving his arms frantically.

The horse and wagon narrowly missed the cement. The eggman teetered, seemed to hover, then regained his balance. The milkman came to an abrupt halt, cursing and muttering, 'That kid scared my horse! Whoa . . ! Whoa . . ! Victoria . . . whoa!' Victoria raced on, ignoring his cries.

A dandy pedalling along the narrow street on his bicycle swerved to avoid the terror-stricken horse. It was a bad move. He headed right for Elliott. Pete knew what would happen when the dandy hit an invisible barrier. He tried to yell a warning.

'Look out! Go the other way!'

The dandy was too full of his own importance as he tipped his hat to two ladies walking on the opposite side of the street. He had no intention of listening to a grubby street urchin. The next moment he had run full tilt into Elliott. The dragon was not hurt, but the dandy was thrown from his bike and landed heavily on the dusty street. For a long moment he lay in stunned silence. When he picked himself up he glared angrily at Pete as he brushed dirt from his coat.

'You should've gotten out of the way,' said Pete feeling rather guilty. 'I'm sorry, sir. Elliott didn't mean to . . .' He bit back the rest of the sentence.

The dandy's ego was bruised, as well as his body. He had been made to appear foolish in front of the ladies he had hoped to impress. They were giggling quietly into their handkerchiefs. 'You made me fall . . . waving your arms like that!' he snarled at Pete.

'Oh no, sir . . . it wasn't . . .' Pete turned to Elliott who was grinning. 'Don't just stand there – do something,' he ordered the dragon.

Elliott did. Obligingly, he righted the bicycle. To the observer, the action was uncanny. The bike righted itself. Pete was nowhere near it. The bike's owner could only stare, his mouth hanging open. Questions formed in his mind but before he had uttered a word he was lifted in mid-air, then dropped onto the seat of his bicycle. He gripped the handlebars, his knuckles showing white, his face a picture of shocked surprise. As a final goodwill gesture, Elliott picked up the man's hat and placed it on his head. Across the street, the two ladies nudged each other. Something very odd was going on.

Pete whispered, 'That's better, Elliott. Now get him rolling again.'

The dragon was not taking life too seriously and mischievously shoved the dandy and his bike backwards. The startled man sailed along a garden path and into a house with an open door. From the shadowy hall came an ominous crash.

A distraught householder waved his arms and shouted at the dandy, 'Don't ride through my house with that contraption.'

Muttering apologies the terrified man rode off in the opposite direction. He had decided to go back to bed and start all over again. This was certainly not his day.

By now, Pete was thoroughly alarmed. Elliott's behaviour had attracted far too much attention and Pete knew that he would be blamed. 'I told you to get him rolling, but not backwards,' he grumbled. 'Why can't you think before you do things?'

Elliott made a small sound expressing his apologies.

The two ladies exchanged meaningful glances and one of them asked, 'Who are you talking to, boy?'

'Oh . . . er . . . I'm just talking to my dragon, Elliott,' he explained.

They didn't wait to question Pete further. Convinced that he was crazy, they hoisted their long skirts and ran squealing down the street.

Pete watched them go, a worried frown creasing his forehead. His voice was low and stern as he told Elliott, 'No more fooling around. Stay next to me.'

Pete retraced his steps taking care as he passed the wet cement not to walk on it. Unfortunately, Elliott was not so careful. Dragon footprints formed a pattern right through the centre and the dazed cement man was so stunned that he could not make a sound. He collapsed weakly on the sidewalk attempting to persuade himself that he was suffering from hallucinations.

Pete edged towards a hardware store. Elliott followed, not watching where he was going and banged his head on the sign swinging above the shop. One of the hinges snapped and the sign fell sideways, swaying in the breeze. The angry proprietor rushed through his front door, his face red with anger.

Pete sighed. 'I told you to look out, Elliott!' Now, it was too late; the damage was done. Pete, his eyes still fixed on the broken sign, stepped warily back. It was back luck that he was on a direct collision course with Miss Taylor, a prim, prissy school-teacher.

'Look out,' she snapped as she and Pete bumped into each other. 'Clumsy! Clumsy!' she said savagely glaring at this scruffy boy who had dared to come in contact with her.

'I'm sorry! Real sorry!' murmured Pete.

Miss Taylor, dressed in a brown hat and a full cape which reached her ankles pulled herself up to her full height, narrowed her eyes and said haughtily, 'People shouldn't look up at the sky when they walk.'

Pete ventured to explain. 'I was telling my dragon not to bump his head on the sign.' He pointed to it.

Miss Taylor's students were grouped behind their teacher. Pete's remark sent them into peals of laughter. She spun round glaring at them each in turn. The smiles were instantly erased as the children assumed dead-pan expressions.

'All right, smarties,' announced Miss Taylor in icy tones. 'To your classroom . . . march, march, march!'

Disappointed, yet not daring to disobey, the pupils marched briskly in orderly columns to the schoolhouse. Miss Taylor watched, her grey eyes cold as steel. 'March . . . march . . .' she ordered. When they were out of earshot she directed her attention again to Pete. 'How dare you . . . I mean, how dare you lie to me, and try to embarrass me in front of my students?'

Pete had not lied but of course, Miss Taylor could not see the dragon. 'I'm not lying,' he complained.

'That's a lie on top of a lie. You're not one of my pupils. What school are you playing hookey from?'

Pete looked miserable and stammered, 'I . . . I don't go to school.' He wished that he did but the Gogans had never given time off for a formal education.

'I knew it!' Miss Taylor stuck her nose in the air. 'You're just what this town needs . . . another ignoramus. Shoo . . . shoo . . .' She waved her arms as if brushing away an insect, turned on her heels and stalked off.

Her high-handed manner was too much for the indignant Elliott.

He instantly decided that she needed a lesson in manners and hooked her long skirt onto a large nail protruding from a packing crate . . . right beside Pete.

Pete saw Elliott's action, lunged desperately to free the fabric but was not in time. There was a loud ripping sound and Miss Taylor's skirt was whipped off, revealing her pantaloons. She shrieked, furious and humiliated.

'You disgusting little street urchin,' she shrilled. 'You'll be locked up for this! Where's the Sheriff?'

'Please . . .!' Pete ran forward, pleading. 'I didn't do anything. Your skirt got caught on a nail.'

'Yes . . . your fingernail!' she snorted. 'Give me that!' Viciously, she tore the skirt from his hands, ripping the fabric completely. With as much dignity as she could muster, she strode towards the school, her cheeks flaming.

The incident had amused Elliott and he grinned – a wide, invisible grin – and rocked a maypole within easy reach of his height. 'Elliott, stop that!' cried Pete in despair. His morning had been a disaster from the time they first entered the village. Now, the angry residents were closing in. Pete was scared.

'That kid scared my horse!' yelled the milkman.

'He ruined my cement!'

'Look what he did to my sign!' cried the hardware proprietor, dancing with indignation.

Pete didn't wait to hear the full list of complaints. He turned and ran. If only that had been the end of the shambles but . . .

The Mayor, a large, imposing man who clearly thought a great deal of himself, emerged from the town hall, closely followed by two of his commissioners. The Mayor was rehearsing a speech and as he descended the town hall steps he quoted: 'Passamaquoddy is a peaceful community, upon which the sun rises . . . and . . . the sun sets. That's very deep, isn't it?' he asked his men.

The commissioners hastened to agree.

The Mayor was totally absorbed. 'And then I'll say, It's a place of serenity and security. A place where the unexpected never happens. A place that says . . . Welcome!' He spread his arms in a ceremonial gesture and closed his eyes.

He was in for a rude awakening.

Pete turned to summon Elliott and fell over the eggman who had given chase. The eggman lost his balance and slammed into the Mayor. Eggs flew in all directions, broken eggs, whole eggs, egg-whites, egg-yolks; they splattered everywhere but in particular over the Mayor, covering him from head to foot and welding him to the eggman in one gigantic scramble.

It was too much! Pete was horrified. 'Let's get out of here, Elliott,' he gasped . . . and ran.

Elliott thought the picture was hilarious, especially the Mayor and the eggman trying to separate themselves from each other. Stuck up . . . and stuck together. The dragon almost fell over laughing.

Wrathful cries echoed along the street after Pete's fleeing form.

'It was that kid what pushed me!'

'He scared my Victoria!'

'He pulled off Miss Taylor's skirt!'

'He walked through my cement with his big feet!'

'Where *is* this person?' demanded the Mayor pompously, flicking egg-yolk from his lapel.

'There he goes!' Eager arms pointed in Pete's direction.

'Detain him,' bellowed the Mayor. How dare anyone upset the peace and tranquillity of Passamaquoddy!

Chapter Three

Breathless and scared, Pete rushed past a tavern close to the waterfront and ducked out of sight. His breath came in hard, short gasps as he looked around frantically for a better place to hide. Spying a pile of crates he darted behind them. Minutes later his pursuers thundered by, yelling furiously.

'Who's responsible for my eggs?' gasped the eggman as they drew level with Pete.

'Your hens,' puffed the red-faced Mayor, and on they went.

Pete listened anxiously and when he could no longer hear their pounding feet he turned to speak to Elliott. He had no difficulty finding the dragon. Elliott had materialised and as he looked down at Pete from his great height he grinned soppily.

'Elliott!' Pete choked, close to tears. 'You spoiled everything!'

Elliott had the grace to look guilty.

Exasperated, Pete shook his finger. 'I told you to behave!'

The green dragon shrugged. He couldn't help being mischievous once in a while: but it did always seem to get Pete into trouble.

At that moment the door of the tavern swung open and a man staggered onto the street. Laughing, teetering uncertainly, he wiped a froth of beery foam from his mouth. Pete cautiously popped his head above a crate and looked at the seaman . . . at least, he was dressed like one. He was a short man and had a jovial, rollicking air. His complexion was sunburned and on his chin he had a white, stubbly growth. His peaked cap was turned sideways.

The old man lumbered round the corner and Pete ducked down. Too late. The man had spotted him. Grinning widely he said in a friendly tone, 'Hiya, kid!'

'Hi!' responded Pete. It was the first friendly greeting he had received since entering the village of Passamaquoddy.

The man, known to his friends as Lampie, smiled again. Then he saw Elliott! He rubbed his eyes and peered glassily at the green dragon. 'Hiya! Say . . . you look terrible.' He jerked his thumb in Elliott's direction and whispered to Pete, 'Hey, kid . . . your friend turned green!' He blinked, his face frozen in sudden shock, his voice trailed away. Shaking like a leaf in a storm he stammered, 'D-d-dragon! It's a dragon!' Terrified, he backed away, turned and charged back into the saloon. Pink elephants he had known – but green dragons? Never! He needed another drink . . . a stiff one!

Pete bit his lip when the drunk had gone. 'Didn't I tell you to . . .'
Elliott did try to look sorry, and discreetly disappeared again.

Lampie's dramatic re-entry into the smoke-filled tavern did not
cause the faintest flicker of interest even when he shouted at the
top of his lungs, 'Dragons! Dragons! Street's full of dragons!'

The customers smiled, winked, nudged each other and returned
to their drinking. The clientele of the waterfront saloon were well
used to Lampie's drunken illusions. He was the local lighthouse-
keeper and it was an accepted fact that when on duty he could be
relied upon to do what was demanded of him . . . and remain
sober. His leisure time . . . well . . . that was another matter. Nora,
his pretty young daughter could handle him.

With the memory of the green dragon still vivid, Lampie strove
again to warn his fellow drinkers. They were unimpressed and
continued to play cards, joke, and above all . . . drink. Soon, Nora
would come in search of her father and take him home to sleep off
the remnants of his daytime nightmare.

Undaunted by the indifference of his comrades, Lampie dashed
into the centre of the floor and in a loud voice sang:

> 'A dragon, a dragon,
> I swear I saw a dragon.
> A green and seething, fire-breathing
> Monster is in sight,
> With eyes of red, a lion's head
> And wings as dark as night!
> Oh, he has a jaw of gleaming teeth,
> He's fifty feet in height!
> It's true, it's true,
> Oh, what are we to do?
> It's true, it's true,
> He'll break us all in two!
> Oh, he's coming in –
> A gret big fin
> Is right against the door,
> So board up all the windows
> And get down on the floor.'

Lampie had nearly frightened himself to death with his song, so
when the tavern door suddenly swung open, he shrieked in terror
and dived under a table.

It was not a dragon who walked into the smoke-filled saloon but
a pretty young lady. Dressed in her working clothes she wore a
checked blouse, a long skirt and a pair of boots. She was quite
lovely with curly chestnut hair, large tawny brown eyes and a

creamy complexion. Her eyes twinkled as she asked cheerily, 'Anyone seen my dad?'

Lampie crawled from beneath the table and gesticulated wildly. 'Nora . . . Nora . . . get away from the door . . . quick!'

Quizzically, Nora asked, 'What's happening?'

Lampie staggered to his feet, his face a mask of fear. 'Saw something terrible . . . worst I ever saw in my life. Right out there on the street.' He collapsed weakly into a chair.

'What was it?' Nora was frankly puzzled.

'Hate to tell you . . . don't want to scare you,' muttered Lampie darkly, his voice slurred with drink.

'Scare me?' Nora smiled kindly at her father. She was used to his whims and flights of fancy.

Lampie screwed up his eyes, and broke into song:

> 'A dragon, a dragon,
> I swear I saw a dragon,
> His tail lashing, see him smashing
> Every shop in town,
> With scaly feet he cracked the street
> And tore the steeple down.
> It's not some loony dream, I heard
> A *scream* from Sheriff Brown.
> It's true, it's true,
> Oh, what are we to do?
> It's true, it's true . . .'

The customers at the bar mockingly, took up the chant:

> 'Oh, Lampie's in a stew!
> A dragon, a dragon,
> Oh, Lampie saw a dragon.
> He's bleary-eyed, he's ossified,
> He's tighter than a tick.
> He had too much to drink today,
> So call a doctor, quick!'

Nora's eyes flashed angrily. She disliked the men ridiculing her father and reached for old Lampie's arm.

> 'I'd better take him home to bed
> Before you make him sick!'

Lampie cried:

'We're sunk, we're sunk!'

The men chanted:

> 'Go on with you, you're drunk!
> A dragon, a dragon,
> He says he saw a dragon.'

Nora stamped her foot and sang:

> 'The game is done, you've had your fun,
> My dad's been through enough.
> So won't you all behave yourselves,
> I don't want any guff.
> You're like a bunch of little boys
> Who play at being tough!
> You'll see, you'll see,
> You've met your match in me!'

Lampie took up the song:

> 'Oh, you always jeer and laugh and sneer,
> But look across the square.'

The jocular customers humoured Lampie:

> 'All right, we'll go and take a look
> Good Lord, Good Lord,
> There's absolutely nothing anywhere!'

Lampie refused to believe them.

> 'It *was* there!
> A dragon, a dragon,
> I swear I saw a dragon.'

The rest of the customers chorused:

> 'You're off your hinges, all those binges
> Put you in a haze.'

Nora leapt onto the counter and danced along the bar, her tawny eyes flashing angrily:

> 'You crazy fools, it's all your doggone

Fault he's in a daze.
Let go of me, let go of me,
And mend your wicked ways.'

Laughing and winking the men replied:

'What makes you think there ever was?
You know there never never never
Never never never never
Never never never was a dragon!'

From her vantage point on the bar counter Nora had a clear
view. The crowd was growing restive. Men were rising from the
tables and jostling each other in the smoky atmosphere. A brawny
fisherman gave Lampie a good-natured push, but it was enough to
spark off trouble. To divert attention from her father, Nora knocked
the stoppers out of the kegs of beer lined up at each end of the
counter. Foam gushed from the kegs and in the ensuing confusion,
Nora leapt to the ground, grabbed her father and hastily propelled
him outside the tavern.

Once outside the murky saloon, Nora shook her chestnut curls
and breathed in the salty, invigorating air. Her father stumbled
along ahead of her. Nora watched him and smiled tolerantly. She
readily forgave her father his weakness for drink, but this was the
first time he had ever talked about *dragons*! She hoped he would not
persist.

Lampie staggered towards the lighthouse calling over his
shoulder, 'This was the real thing, I'm tellin' you. Big monster . . .
with wings . . . smoke comin' from its nostrils . . . just standin'
there, outside the saloon.'

'It was probably waiting for someone to buy it a drink,' replied
Nora flippantly.

'Don't make fun of me! I'm telling you there really is a dragon!'
Lampie lurched angrily through the front door of the lighthouse.

Nora gave an indulgent shrug and followed. Her father needed
a sound sleep before she would get any sense out of him. Even from
a distance she could smell the alcoholic fumes which resulted from
his morning's revels.

Inside the lighthouse, Nora led her father gently into his
bedroom. Lampie groaned and flung himself onto his bunk,
dishevelled and disappointed. No-one would believe him. Nora
made him comfortable, tucked the covers round his chin and crept
from the room. Already, he was half asleep, and still muttering
about the mysterious dragon.

'It's face . . . if you call it a face . . . was this close to me!' He lifted one arm to demonstrate.

From the doorway, Nora said, 'Go to sleep now, Dad.'

Lampie moved his head to one side. 'Funny thing . . . it sort of smiled at me . . .'

Nora re-entered the room and sat on the side of her father's bunk. 'And did you smile back?' she asked, her tawny eyes twinkling humorously.

'My feet were movin' too fast. There was this boy . . . standin' next to it . . . didn't seem to be afraid . . . Yeah . . . this boy . . .' Lampie's voice trailed away on a note of wonder.

Nora smoothed his pillow. 'I'll take the first watch,' she told him. 'You can tell me about it later, when you take the midnight watch. Sleep now.' Bending over her father, Nora kissed his forehead and his eyes closed. As she shut the bedroom door, Lampie was still muttering about the dragon.

Smiling, Nora moved into another room. She paused in front of a mahogany chest of drawers on which stood a photograph of a handsome, dark-haired young man dressed in a seaman's uniform. His eyes appeared to be staring directly at her. She shivered, her face clouding. Suddenly, the vibrant chestnut-haired girl looked vulnerable and lonely. She stared for a long time at the face of the man she loved. Paul was a seaman born in Passamaquoddy. She and Paul had had an understanding. Everybody had expected them to be married. But then Paul had failed to return from a voyage and by now it seemed certain that he had drowned at sea. Nora blinked back a flood of hot tears. Then she shook herself mentally; there was important work to do . . . other seamen's lives to consider.

Slowly, she climbed the circular staircase of the lighthouse. Soon the sun would set and it would be time for her to begin her watch. When she reached the lantern-house she lit the wicks, set the machinery in motion and watched the giant lens rotate. A brilliant beam of light flashed seawards. Satisfied that all was in good working order she moved outside onto the narrow gallery that ran all round the circular lighthouse. A stiff breeze raked her curls as she watched the tide coming in from her high vantage point. The sea was grey and choppy and the dark clouds gathering on the horizon promised a stormy night ahead.

Feeling restless and depressed, Nora decided to take a stroll along the cliffs.

After Lampie's brief encounter with Elliott outside the tavern, Pete had been forced to remain in hiding. Now, daylight was fading as

he and Elliott rambled aimlessly along the sandy beach. Pete was dejected. He looked a sorry sight, ragged, tired and dirty. All his life he had been abused, suffered blows, kicks and curses, and freedom was still a novelty, but what he felt most now were the sharp pangs of hunger. He stumbled over the craggy rocks and a huge wave washed over him, drenching him to the skin. A cold wind blew off the water and he shivered.

Things might have been different if Elliott had not misbehaved. He stared stonily at the dragon. 'I told you not to show yourself,' he said, his small voice forlorn.

Elliott looked penitent and in an attempt to please Pete, made himself disappear.

Pete was not impressed. Moodily, he kicked a pebble. Everyone in Passamaquoddy hated him now; he didn't dare show his face there again. How could he hope for a kind word, a friendly gesture? From where he stood the world seemed huge and hostile. He dug his hands into his pockets but there wasn't any happy jingle of coins . . . only a series of holes in the lining.

Peering through the gloom, Pete noticed a cave, its entrance yawning like a cavernous black mouth. At least it might provide shelter . . . of a sort. He headed towards it and it was at that exact moment that Nora, higher up along the cliffs noticed the boy down on the sandy shore. She frowned and when he entered the cave she sprinted back to the lighthouse for a lantern. At high tide, the cave was sometimes flooded.

Pete groped his way inside the cave. He could barely see and he had to wait for his eyes to become accustomed to the gloom. Gripped by panic, he tried to hide his fear. The place was shadowy and slippery with seaweed. Pete sneezed twice and fumbled for a place to sit down. What was he going to do? Where would he go tomorrow? He sneezed again and shivered violently.

Elliott materialised again and made a sound, soft and sympathetic. The dragon was worried. Pete was in a bad way. In an effort to cheer him up, the dragon gathered together some pieces of driftwood and blowing a brilliant flame from his nostrils, managed to light a small fire. Using a charred stick he drew noughts and crosses over the tough hide of his tummy and offered the stick to Pete. A game should cheer him up.

Pete was clearly not in the mood for games. Irritably, he pushed the stick aside, muttering, 'I don't want to play.'

Elliott's friendly gesture had been rejected and the dragon was hurt. Perhaps if he tried again . . .

His second effort brought a stinging accusation. 'We're in a lot of trouble, and it's all your fault!'

Elliott blinked and looked guilty. He hadn't meant to make trouble for his young companion. Somehow, it had just happened.

'You did everything wrong in Passamaquoddy. Now everybody hates us.' Pete sniffed, unable to stifle his tears. Between sobs he blurted, 'I don't know whether you're good for me . . . or bad.'

Elliott hung his head in shame. By nature a friendly, lovable, though mischievous creature, he wished desperately that he could put things right. But how? He put another X and an O on his tummy, trying to look cheerful and penitent at the same time.

Pete rubbed his nose and wiped his eyes. 'I'm sorry, Elliott,' he apologised, his expression softening. 'It's just that I don't know what to do . . . and I'm scared.' The roar of the surf pounded in their ears and spray broke inside the cave. Even the eerie shadows seemed to whisper a message of menace.

A big, solitary tear trickled slowly down Pete's cheek. Elliott watched the tear sparkling like a dew drop at dawn. He leaned down, and gently . . . very gently caught it in his claw. For a long moment he studied the gleaming droplet then shyly offered Pete the charred stick again. It was Elliott's way of saying he was sorry. This time, Pete accepted the stick. The two odd friends started to play noughts and crosses. What else was there to do?

'Hello in there . . .'

The unexpected sound of a human voice was so shattering that Pete literally jumped . . . then scampered for a place to hide. Elliott, too, dashed behind a rock, one eye peering round the corner.

Pete was not fast enough. As Nora stepped cautiously into the cave holding a bright lantern, Pete was caught in its rays. 'Hi. What are you doing here?' she asked.

Pete tried to act casually as though hiding in a cave was an ordinary, everyday occurrence. 'Oh . . . just playing noughts and crosses,' he murmured.

Nora showed her surprise. There wasn't anyone else in the cave to play with. 'This isn't the best place for noughts and crosses,' she advised. 'The tide's coming in and high water reaches this cave sometimes. Better head for home.'

Pete bit his lower lip and turned his head away. If only he had a decent home to go to!

Nora was quick to note his reaction. 'You're not from Passamaquoddy, are you?' she asked.

Pete shook his head. 'Nope. Just sort of . . . travelling.' His voice trailed off.

'Where are your parents?'

Pete shrugged.

Nora's concern mounted as she eyed his wet clothes. 'Where are you staying? What's your name?'

He ignored the first question and answered the second. 'Pete!'

As he glanced shyly up at her in the flickering light, her heart immediately went out to the cold, lonely little boy. Another wave broke outside the cave and this time the spray came right over their feet.

Nora made a swift decision, and introduced herself. 'I'm Nora. I have to get back on watch, up in the lighthouse. There's chowder on the stove . . . if you'd like some . . .'

For a moment, Pete hesitated with his natural distrust of people. Then his stomach growled angrily, and the hunger pains made him feel faint. Slowly, he nodded his head and moved towards her. Nora smiled and reached out her hand. Reluctant, Pete touched it briefly then pulled back. No-one had ever made a truly friendly gesture before – except Elliott – and he was unsure of himself . . . and of Nora.

She was frankly puzzled. 'Hey . . . what's the matter? It's a hand . . . not a shark.' Suspicion and fear showed clearly on the boy's face. Nora promised, 'You can finish off the chowder if you'd like.'

Pete's blue gaze studied her. She was pretty . . . and she looked kind. Slowly, offering his trust, he extended his hand. Holding it firmly, she squeezed it and smiled. Together, they moved to the mouth of the cave.

They were walking steadily along the sand keeping well back from the long-fingered surf when Pete stopped dead in his tracks. 'I forgot something,' he blurted out. 'Be right back.'

Before Nora could protest he had dashed away.

Inside the cave, Pete stumbled on a slimy rock as he called, 'Elliott!' The dragon lumbered forward expecting to accompany Pete. The boy shook his head. 'No, no. Not yet. Stay here while I see what it's like up at the lighthouse.' Barely able to see, he picked up a stick and drew an X on the dragon's tummy and put a line through it. The move tickled Elliott and he uttered a low, rumbling laugh. Pete blew him a kiss before rushing back along the beach to his new friend.

Elliott watched Pete until he couldn't see him any more, then retreated to the back of the cave to make himself as comfortable as possible – under the circumstances.

Nora ushered Pete inside the lighthouse and while the clam chowder was warming on the stove she poured water into an enamel bowl, gave Pete a sponge and a towel and told him to wash his face and hands. A bath could come later. Pete felt a sense of amazement. The Gogans had never made him wash and the only times he had ever looked fairly clean was after Willie or Grover had ducked him in the farm pond. Pete rubbed lots of soap onto the sponge and washed with enthusiasm. It was a new experience. When he saw the film of dirty scum floating on the water's surface he felt a sense of shame. Nora only laughed and went to fetch a hairbrush.

Minutes later, Pete was seated at a stout table, his face clean, his eyes shining and his red hair neatly brushed. It was a transformation. Nora had produced a pair of over-sized pyjamas belonging to her father and Pete was wearing them. For the first time in his life he felt clean and comfortable.

Nora poured some thick, creamy soup into a deep bowl as Pete's eyes darted round the room taking in all the details. He looked with a sense of wonder at the polished oak dresser holding an assortment of shining brass lanterns and pretty china teapots. A carved oak chest stood in one corner next to a grandfather clock with a loud, solemn tick, and a gaily coloured rug covered the floor. It was the cosiest, prettiest room Pete had ever seen. Most exciting was the long, curving staircase winding up and up. It would be fun to explore.

Nora placed the appetising chowder in front of him and for the next few moments Pete's whole attention was absorbed in eating. He was famished. He emptied the bowl and wordlessly, Nora gave him a second generous helping. At last, Pete had eaten his fill and he pushed away the bowl and put down his spoon. Then he glanced candidly at Nora who was watching him, compassion written on her lovely face.

Nora chose this moment to ask him the question that had been bothering her ever since she had found him: where did he come from?

Pete shrugged. 'The Gogans own me, I guess. They said it was against the law for me to ever leave them.'

Nora gently traced the outline of a bruise, now clearly visible on his freckled face. 'Where did you get that bruise?' she asked with kindly concern.

'Mr Gogan!' said Pete matter-of-factly. 'I was milking the cow and I missed the bucket.' So used to abuse, he showed no particular resentment.

Nora's expression darkened. 'Had he done that before?'

Pete rested his chin on his hands. 'All the time. The orphan home sent me back the first time I ran away. This time . . . I'll just keep running.'

Nora felt an immediate sense of outrage and indignation against the pitiless Gogans. She was torn with pity for Pete's plight. 'You'll be safe here,' she said firmly.

Pete stared deep into Nora's tawny eyes. He liked her . . . really liked her. 'Nora . . . no-one's ever been this nice to me,' he murmured. 'I'll always remember it. Thank you!'

Nora had swiftly considered the situation. 'Pete . . . you'd better stay here tonight,' she offered. 'We'll figure out what to do tomorrow. Okay?'

Pete's hesitation was fractional then he nodded, smiling. A strange new happiness stole over him. Suddenly, he didn't feel lonely any more.

'Wonderful,' responded Nora. 'Come on,' she held out her hand, 'I've got to trim the wicks.'

This time there was no hesitation over Pete taking her hand and he climbed the spiralling stairs with curiosity.

'Are you anybody's mother?' he asked as they climbed.

A tinge of regret coloured Nora's voice. 'I'm not even anybody's wife.'

'But you're gonna get married and all, aren't you?' persisted Pete.

'I'm already married to this lighthouse.' She smiled, trying to look cheerful.

'Who's that?' Pete pointed to the photograph of the young man in seaman's clothing for they had reached a niche halfway up the stairs where there was a small room.

'Paul,' replied Nora.

'Is he part of your family?'

Nora seemed to be a long time in answering. 'He almost was . . .' She sighed.

Pete's curiosity got the better of him. 'How can someone almost be a part of a family?'

Nora continued walking up the stairs, Pete at her heels. 'We were . . . going to be married.'

They reached the top of the stairs and Nora busied herself trimming the wicks, her usually smiling face serious.

'How come you weren't?' queried Pete.

Nora's sigh this time was audible. 'As far as we know, his ship was headed into a storm. They were never heard from again. That was a year ago.'

'He'll come back,' said Pete, his young firm voice full of confidence.

Nora's hand was shaking as she turned away from the gleaming lights. How many times had she prayed for just such a miracle? 'That's what I say every day as I stand up here watching ships on the horizon. Time I started thinking about other things . . . so they tell me.'

She moved back to the stairs. Pete followed, silent and deep in thought. As they were descending the twisting stairwell he said, 'I'll have to ask Elliott about Paul. He has a way of knowing things.'

Nora's brows drew together in a fine, dark line. 'Who is Elliott?'

'My dragon!'

'Dragon . . .?' A little smile plucked at the corners of her mouth. 'Oh . . . so you're the one with the dragon.'

'Yup!'

'Where is he?' asked Nora, humouring her little stray boy.

'Down the cave.'

'I see,' she said as they came back into the cosy living room. Nora sat at a sewing table, and Pete dropped onto a stool beside her.

'That's interesting,' said Nora picking up her mending. 'I've never known anyone with a dragon. What does he look like?'

'Just a plain ordinary dragon.' Pete stretched.

'How plain? How ordinary?' persisted Nora.

Pete grinned. He knew the best way to describe Elliott. He broke into song:

> 'He has the head of a camel,
> The neck of a crocodile.'

Nora retaliated:

> 'It sounds rather strange.'

Pete replied:

> 'He's both a fish and a mammal,
> And I hope he'll never change,
> 'Cause it's not easy
> To find someone who cares.'

Nora agreed:

> 'It's not easy
> To find magic in pairs.'

Pete laughed:

> 'I'm glad I found him, I love him,
> I won't let him get away,
> 'Cause it's not easy . . .'

Nora was puzzled:

> 'You say the head of a camel,
> The neck of a crocodile.'

Pete nodded enthusiastically:

> 'And the ears of a cow!'

Nora, half accepting these explanations, continued:

> 'It's clear that friends can be different.
> Yes, I understand you now!'

In harmony, Pete and Nora sang:

> 'It's not easy
> To find someone who cares.
> It's not easy
> To find magic in pairs.'

Nora advised:

> 'Now that you have him, hold him,
> Treasure him from day to day.
> It's so easy . . .
> Life is lollipops and raindrops
> With the one you love –
> Someone you can always be with,
> Argue and agree with –'

Pete cut in:

> 'Climb the highest tree with!'

They sang together:

> 'It's not easy
> To share somebody's dream.
> It gets easy
> When you work as a team.'

Alone, Nora crooned:

> 'You've got to tend it, fan it . . .'

Pete replied:

> 'That's what I plan to do.
> Oh, I had one friend by my side.
> Now I have two –
> Him and you!'

Nora laughed:

> 'Him and me.'

In harmony they chorused:

> 'And it's so easy!'

Nora's eyes crinkled with laughter and Pete joined in. Then he yawned . . . a big, wide yawn. Nora pointed to a bunk she had made up in readiness. Tired, happy, secure, Pete climbed into the comforting warmth of the downy blankets. Nora kissed him lightly on the forehead, tucked in the patchwork quilt and turned the lamp low. Then she picked up her sewing again.

She would have been surprised . . . even shocked . . . if she had glanced over her shoulder. Elliott was peering through the window, a smile of approval on his big, soppy face.

Chapter Four

A bell clanging inside the lighthouse announced that it was midnight. Lampie, sober now but still suffering from the effects of his morning's drinking, staggered uncertainly up the circular stairs to the watchroom. He gained the top step, looked as though he was about to lose his balance, but managed to grasp the top rail just in time. Through a haze, he saw Nora and saluted.

'Changing the watch, my love!' he boomed. Lampie prided himself on never missing a watch . . . hung-over or not.

'How do you feel, Dad?' asked Nora kindly.

'In the pink . . . in the pink,' Lampie assured her. A foghorn shrieked and the loud blast set Lampie's teeth on edge. Gingerly, he touched his aching temples. Drumming pain pulsated through his whole head. He shuddered. 'I'll never do my six hours with that noise going on.'

Nora said, 'You'll make it,' and poured him a cup of steaming coffee. Lampie drank the dark brew and glanced around the small room. He shook his head at a line of washing drying close to the stove.

'Kitchen's gettin' the look of a laundry . . . rags hangin' there.'

Nora looked at the freshly washed, shoddy garments which had passed for Pete's clothing. 'We've a guest, a young boy . . . a runaway orphan,' she told her father. 'I'd like him to stay, if it's all right.'

Lampie tenderly scratched his aching head. 'Sure . . . sure he can.'

A faint snore issued from the bunk where Pete lay asleep. Lampie raised one expressive eyebrow. That was all he needed. 'It'll be some night, between him and the foghorn,' he grumbled. To have a hangover was bad enough in itself; to share it with a noisy foghorn and a snoring boy . . . Where was there justice in the world? Draining his coffee cup he commenced his watch.

Pete woke early the next morning. He felt wonderfully rested and had just enjoyed his best night's sleep ever. The morning sun flung a shower of gold through the window and he sat up, rubbing his eyes and blinking. As he swung his feet over the side of the bunk, Lampie turned. He did not immediately recognise Pete – but Pete recognised Lampie.

'Hello, lad.' Lampie's smile was warm and welcoming.

Pete dropped to the floor. 'Hello, sir. Nice to see you again!'

Lampie hadn't heard that remark. 'You sure gave the foghorns fair competition last night,' he joked and imitated Pete's loud snore. Pete laughed infectiously and watched the old man moving about the room putting everything ship-shape. 'Why, anytime we need a replacement for the old horns, we'll just . . .' Lampie looked hard at Pete. This time he remembered. His eyes bulged and he yelled. 'Yaaaaa! It's you! It's you! Yaaaa!' He backed away from Pete as memories of yesterday returned to haunt him. 'You're the one with the . . . dragon . . .?'

'Yes, sir,' answered Pete, quite mystified. Why was Lampie making such a fuss? Elliott wouldn't harm him. Pete knew that the dragon had liked the old man.

'W-w-w-where is it?' Lampie's voice shook.

'Down below, sir.'

Lampie looked horrified. Rushing to the stairwell he poked his head over the rail. There wasn't a dragon in sight but Nora was running swiftly up the stairs, her face tense. 'Dad. Dad . . . What is it?' Her father's screams had been audible on the beach above the surf.

Lampie pointed at Pete, his face pale. 'It's . . . it's . . . him!' He spoke dramatically, then dropped his voice to a whisper. 'The one with the *dragon!*'

Nora thought her father had suddenly gone quite crazy. She attempted to humour him. 'I know . . . I know. Now just take it easy.' She led him to a chair and forced him to sit down.

'Did you see it? Did you see it?' repeated Lampie, his eyes darting nervously round the small room.

Nora played her little game. 'I didn't actually see it . . . but I know what it looks like. We'll talk about it . . . later.'

Lampie was not to be put off. He peered over his shoulder. 'I just want to know . . . is the thing in the lighthouse?'

Pete answered that question. 'No. Elliott's down in the cave.'

Lampie frowned. 'You mean . . . it's even got a name?'

'There's nothing to get upset about,' cut in Nora soothingly.

A sudden thought struck Lampie and he leapt to his feet. Now, he could prove his point. No-one had believed him yesterday. 'You're right,' he told his daughter. 'I shouldn't be upset . . . I should be happy. Yes . . . happy . . . because all I gotta do is show him to the guys in the saloon. Then you'll hear the apologies.'

Pete beamed. 'Elliott'll be happy to do it for you, sir.'

'Good lad, good lad. You, me and Elliott'll march right into the tavern when it opens. Can't wait to see their faces.' He asked nervously, 'Elliott . . . he won't scratch or bite or start a fire, will he?'

40

Pete put his head to one side and said uncertainly, 'Well, he is sort of . . . unpredictable!'

Nora felt caught up in this silly game of make-believe. After all, there couldn't possibly be a real dragon. She decided to play along. 'Don't do anything with . . . Elliott. Leave him where he is. It's too dangerous to take him into town. I don't want you to say another word about him to anyone, understand, until we've talked this over.' She fixed her father with unusually stern eyes.

Lampie gave her request a moment's thought. 'Oh . . . okay . . .' he finally agreed. 'It's dangerous . . . that's true.'

Satisfied that the situation was sorted out, Nora clapped her hands, smiled and suggested, 'Now let's have breakfast. The lamp has to be cleaned and the lens polished. Then I want to buy some new clothes for Pete.' Fondly, she ruffled his hair.

Pete's face was radiant as a summer's day as he followed Nora towards the staircase. Breakfast . . . and new clothes, too! He could have cuddled Nora and the lighthouse!

Close to the harbour a retired sea captain eagerly scanned the sparkling blue waters with his telescope. It was a breezy morning though the tide was out. Close to the shore little boats with red and orange sails lazed in the mud waiting for the tide to turn; seagulls darted, fought and screamed noisily in their search for food. The captain was disappointed. There were no ships to be seen on the distant horizon.

He swung his telescope landward and bellowed excitedly, 'Somethin's headed this way!' A man at his elbow clad in a jersey followed the old captain's gaze.

Sure enough, a strange-looking vehicle, half wagon, half ship, was heading into Passamaquoddy. Built on wheels, rigged with a mast and propelled by sails it moved swiftly in the wind. The contraption was no more startling in appearance than the man at its helm. He wore a black top hat banded with red silk, a black cape lined with scarlet which billowed from his shoulders and even from a distance it was possible to see his bushy black whiskers and moustache.

Clinging grimly to the mast was a smaller, sandy-haired man dressed in a grey suit and a straw hat. He looked extremely uncomfortable on his perch for also tied to the central pole was a skeleton. Vividly painted slogans were daubed over the entire vehicle. Without modesty, they advertised the wonders and virtues of one Doctor Terminus and his remarkable patent medicines; the infallible cures for every malady under the sun.

The captain snorted derisively as he read the bold announce-

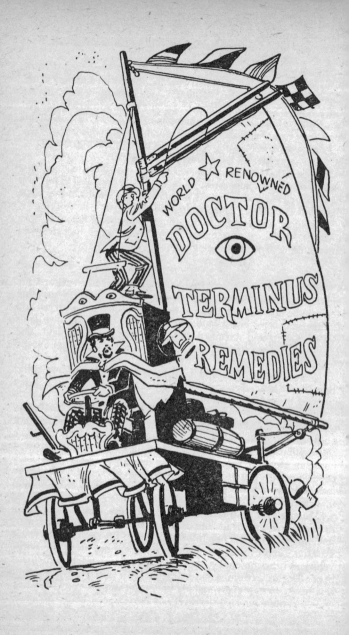

WORLD ★ RENOWNED

DOCTOR

TERMINUS

REMEDIES

ents: DOCTOR TERMINUS . . . WORLD RENOWNED! INSTANT RELIEF
REMEDIES FROM ACROSS THE SEVEN SEAS. *Poppycock*, he thought, and
leaned over the harbour railing to yell in a lusty voice to passers
y, 'Doc Terminus is coming!'

Village folk going quietly about their business looked round;
their expressions immediately changed to contempt and anger.
Doc Terminus had visited them before and the memory returned
ke a black cloud. They remembered how the Doc had tried to
rick and deceive them. He had cheated many out of their hard-
earned money with his phoney remedies. He was the last person
they wanted in Passamaquoddy.

But welcome or not, the doctor had little choice. The wind was
blowing his wagon in the direction of the fishing village and he was
desperate for a refuge, however temporary. An unfriendly mob
rom another community were in hot pursuit, the ungrateful
peasants.

'Hey, Hoagy,' Doc Terminus shouted to his colleague clinging
to the mast. 'They still after us?'

Hoagy peeped nervously over his shoulder. 'Lost 'em,' he called
down. 'Passamaquoddy ahead.'

'What?' cried the doctor swerving and causing the wagon to skid
perilously close to the cliff edge.

Hoagy spelled it out slowly and the doctor heaved a sigh of
esignation. It was most unfortunate that the wind had veered in
his direction. He, too, had unpleasant memories of the village
with the odd-sounding name. The inhabitants had proved unfriendly
just because he had relieved them of a little money . . . well . . .
perhaps more than just a little.

At that precise moment he had another worry to contend with.
He clung desperately to the wheel while trying to reach for the
brake. The wagon was out of control.

'Get the brake,' he yelled up to Hoagy.

Hoagy uttered a small nervous sound and started his wobbly
descent. The mast was high and halfway down he reached the
skeleton. Accidentally he put his hand inside its mouth. The jaws
snapped shut. Hoagy tugged and pulled until finally, with a loud
cry, he and the skeleton hurtled down on top of the irate doctor.

'Get the brake,' pleaded the doctor. 'The brake . . .'

Hoagy seized it with such force that the handle broke in two,
and as the wagon gathered even more speed the doctor clung to his
hat, issuing instructions: 'The wind's making us go faster. Lower
the sail!'

The sea captain's eyes flashed, twin pin-points of angry light.
'All hands on deck,' he warned. 'Here comes the Doc.'

The wagon sideswiped the freshly mended picket fence demolished by Elliott the previous day. Now it lay shattered again. Tears of fury coursed down the face of the unfortunate owner of house and garden. He seemed destined not to keep a fence at all.

'The sail, Hoagy! Lower it!' Terminus was in a panic.

Hoagy with a curious penchant for making any problem multiply itself, got hopelessly tangled in a length of rope. 'The halyard is fouled . . . or something . . .' he squealed miserably. Why did everything he ever touched end up in confusion?

The cement man had already congratulated himself on a job well done, yesterday's damage smoothed over. When he first became aware of the wagon looming on his horizon he knew a moment of righteous indignation . . . then sheer panic. He held up high his sign saying WET CEMENT.

'Wet! Wet! It's still wet!' he shouted, but in vain. The wagon's sail boom swung towards him, he dropped the sign and ran . . right through his cement. The boom struck him in passing knocking him face down in the wet mixture. He raised his head, spitting cement and swearing a terrible vengeance. Then he wept.

'Drop the anchor,' cried Doc Terminus,' before we join the fleet!' They were perilously close to the harbour's edge.

The wagon drew level with the town hall as Hoagy lowered the anchor. It immediately hooked itself onto the town hall steps. They were wooden and the pull on them from the combined weight of the wagon and the anchor whipped them clean away – leaving a long drop.

The Mayor emerged from a meeting, stepped outside and plummeted to the ground like a stone. Considerably shaken he sat up rubbing his bruised torso asking, 'Tell me . . . when did I start losing control of my town?'

The wagon reached the wharf, snagged on a capstan and was jerked to a sharp halt. The jolt clicked a button abruptly catapulting Doc Terminus, Hoagy and the skeleton into a huge fishing net, and transforming the wagon into a clinic and a stage. Yes . . . the residents were left with little doubt that Doc Terminus was back in town!

The disreputable doctor and Hoagy struggled frantically to extricate themselves from the mesh. Already, a crowd of people were rushing towards them.

'You dummy,' hissed the doctor, venting his fury on the luckless Hoagy.

'You told me to drop the anchor,' complained Hoagy, '. . . and I dropped it!'

Doc Terminus sighed and emerged from his mesh trap. One day, Hoagy might do something right. He walked towards the wagon, and Hoagy followed, dragging the skeleton. For the first

44

time the doctor was aware of the threatening expressions on the crowd's faces. He groaned aloud, muttering, 'I think they remember us.'

Hoagy dropped behind by several paces. 'Uh – oh . . . I think I remember them.' His recollections gave him little reason to rejoice.

'Just act normal,' advised the doctor, deciding to bluff his way out of a tricky situation. His entire life was a road of predicaments and he was well used to pulling the wool over people's eyes.

Hoagy shivered. 'I am actin' normal . . . I'm ready to run!' he whispered. His knees felt like jelly.

Using boldness as the best ploy, Doc Terminus leapt onto the stage of his wagon and shamming confidence, beamed at the hostile crowd. 'I can feel the warmth of your welcome permeating the atmosphere. It's so gratifying,' he told them.

A stony silence greeted his remarks. A man at the back of the crowd edged forward growling, 'Get out, ya quack!'

'Don't bring your phoney remedies here again,' retorted another, clenching his fists.

'Go on back where you belong . . . jail!' shrilled a woman pulling her bonnet down more firmly on her grey hair.

'Boo!' chorused the masses.

The situation was more volatile than the doctor had expected. He would have to exert every ounce of charm he possessed – flatter the mob before they turned to violence. He inhaled, then raised his voice above the jeers.

'Thank you, thank you!' he beamed broadly, his eyes twinkling. 'I sense . . . enthusiasm. I sense . . . loving response. That's why I feel this is my home away from home!'

Such audacity brought a low hum of resentment which rapidly grew louder.

Undaunted, the doctor waved his arms and sang:

> 'I've been bringin' cures from Pilgrims'
> Heights to Provincetown.
> Treated rabbit fever down on
> Queen Anne Road.
> Gout or gastritis,
> Mumps or bronchitis,
> Bites and burns and blue abrasions,
> Got a *pill* for all occasions.
> Little Sippewissett
> Was so nice to visit,
> And Scraggy Neck is lovely to recall,
> But through all my trips,
> Good Lord, there's one place,

One corner, one town on my lips –
Why, it's . . .'

Doc Terminus looked anxious. He couldn't recall the name.

'Poddo-ma-quassy . . .'

Glaring faces told him he was wrong.

'Paquo-ma-soddy . . .'

He was wrong again . . . oh dear . . .

'No, no, Passa-ma-massy . . .
Quoda-ma-poddy . . .'

Fear gripped him!

'Passa-ma-daddy . . .
Quoda-ma-passy . . .'

He was almost in tears – hysterical . . .

'Passa-ma-hoddy . . .'

A sudden burst of confidence . . . he must be right this time . . .

'Oh, *I* know. It's Passa-ma-*shloddy*.'

The crowd roared:

'No, it's Passama*quoddy*!'

At last the tension was starting to break. The doctor congratulated himself, grinned and tried wheedling.

'Of course, that's what I *meant* to say.'

A very fat woman stepped to the front of the gaping crowds.

'I took your drug for losing weight,
And now I'm a blob.'

Terminus oozed charm.

46

> 'But now there's so much more
> Of you to love!'

It worked. The fat lady fluttered her eyelashes and looked coy.
A man, his face covered with a red rash complained,

> 'That purple poison ivy pill,
> It ain't done the job.'

The doctor grabbed the man's right hand and inspected it closely.

> 'Why, look at this *hand*,
> It's almost clear.'

Interested, the villagers began to yield a little.
A toothless old man lamented:

> 'You said by spring that I'd be eatin'
> Corn on the cob!'

The doctor thought quickly. This was a tricky one.

> 'Did you take the single,
> Or the double prescription?'

Gummy grandad thought for a moment.

> 'The single only.'

Doc Terminus shrugged, indicating that the double strength should have been used. He spread his hands:

> 'Well . . . what did you *expect*?'

He was well pleased. He almost had the crowd in the palm of his hand. He pressed home his advantage.

> 'I wiped out impetigo on the
> Banks of Buttermilk.
> Flu is under firm control
> In Powder Hole.
> Terminus potions,
> Tablets and lotions,

Major news in modern science –
Step up now and join my clients.
Spent a day in Buzzard's Bay;
They couldn't keep me there.
I *even* turned away from Kingdom Hall.'

The crowds yelled:

'They probably *threw* you out!'

The doctor accepted the retort in high good humour. The spell
was working.

'But since I was young,
Good Lord, there's one spot,
One little bit of heaven on my tongue –
Why it's . . .
Poddo-ma-quassy . . . Paquo-ma-soddy . . .
No, no, Passa-ma-massy . . .
Quoda-ma-poddy . . . Passa-ma-daddy . . .
Quoda-ma-passy . . . Passa-ma-hoddy . . .
Oh, *I* know – it's Passa-ma-*shloddy*.'

Disgruntled, the villagers yelled:

'No, it's Passa-ma-*quoddy*.'

The doctor tittered nervously. He'd have to watch his step.

'Of course, ha, ha, ha,
I knew it all the time!'

A dwarf of a man spoke up.

'You said your pill would make me tall,
And each day I shrink.'

Terminus, happy to act the fool, took a tape measure from his vest
pocket.

'Sir, you're stretching a point –
You've only lost two inches.'

A man in a broad-brimmed hat muttered,

> 'My hair was grey, and thanks to you,
> It's turned into pink!'

He swept off his hat revealing a shock of pink hair. The crowd gasped.

Doctor Terminus replied in a saccharine voice:

> 'But that colour is so becoming!'

The crowd pushed and jostled, closing in on the doctor. They were not to be duped after all. Hoagy, standing quietly in the background took refuge behind a tent flap at the back of the stage.

> 'We're gonna wash your phoney tonics
> Right down the sink.'

The cry unnerved the doctor but he made a last stand.

> 'Wait! Listen! My specialities are –
> Audiology, mycology, serology, Teratology,
> Embryology, Psychology, Zoology . . .
> And any other -ology you can think of.
> Folks, you're not giving me a chance.
> I brought all these medicines back from Paris, France!'

The mob refused to listen, but surged towards the doctor, intent. on revenge. Throwing dignity to the winds he climbed the mast. He prayed for a miracle, and looked around in desperation. Where was Hoagy?

Hoagy, equally afraid, was trying to work a miracle. Behind the tent flap he was hastily disguising himself as an ancient crone. Rapidly, he donned a voluminous dress and a wig, grabbed an enormous ear-trumpet and emerged.

Adopting a quavery voice he called up to the man on the mast, 'Doctor . . . oh, Doctor . . .'

Doc Terminus immediately took up his cue, sliding rapidly down the mast. Hoagy's ruse was one often employed during emergencies.

'I hear someone calling me,' said the doctor sympathetically. 'Someone in need . . . a human being crying out to another human being . . . for a service that only I can provide.' His smile held the milk of human kindness . . . and completely fooled the crowd.

'Madam . . . Doctor Terminus is here to cure you,' he announced.

49

'What . . .? Hoagy shifted the outsize trumpet to his other ear.

The doctor's face darkened as he hopped around to the opposite side and shouted down the trumpet, 'What's the problem, lady?'

'Heh . . .?' Hoagy's pretence of being deaf was perfection.

Terminus appealed to the watching crowd. 'I cannot turn my back on this dear woman.'

Selecting a bottle of medicine from the shelf behind him, he poured half its contents into the ear trumpet. Hoagy swtiched the trumpet over, and the doctor dashed round, pouring the remainder of the liquid into that side. Hoagy put the trumpet down and the wily doctor placed his index fingers inside Hoagy's ears, churning them vigorously. He removed his fingers and stood back.

Hoagy cocked his head, then moved it from side to side. The crowd were fascinated . . . waiting . . .

Hoagy was a master in the art of deceit. He blinked and said in wonderment, 'I hear birds chirping! I hear children giggling! I hear coins jingling! I hear . . . a rhapsody!'

Some-one in the crowd cheered.

'That will be one dollar, please,' announced the doctor holding out his hand in Hoagy's direction.

'Heh?' questioned Hoagy.

'Fifty cents an ear,' explained the doctor, a mischievous smile on his lips.

Hoagy nodded and handed over a coin. 'Bless you, Doctor, bless you!' He hobbled away, anxious to change into his next disguise.

Renewed confidence reverberated in the doctor's voice when he turned to face the audience. 'My medicine cured her! Do you hear her bless me? Well, I bless her, too. How wonderful I feel right in my heart, here!' He placed his hand on his heart. *'Honi soit qui mal y pense!* Shamed be he who thinks evil of it!'

The villagers, though rather wary, could not fail to be impressed.

Hoagy lost no time in dressing up for his next role – that of an old and ailing man. Discreetly, he joined the crowd and almost immediately started to cough . . . a horrid, racking sound. He staggered towards the doctor, hands outstretched, imploring aid.

Terminus looked compassionate. 'What seems to be the trouble, sir?'

Hoagy had another spasm and the doctor made a pretence of listening and diagnosing. 'Aha!' he muttered knowledgeably, and producing a bottle of revolting brown liquid, poured the mixture into Hoagy's open mouth. The cough became a choke . . . a gurgle . . . then there was silence. In the crowd, you could have heard a pin drop.

Hoagy waited a full minute. When he was sure that he had the full attention of everyone present, he broke out into a melodious trill: 'Do-re-mi-fa-sol-la-te-do . . .!' He pretended astonishment, dived into his pocket and gratefully placed another coin into the doctor's hand. Several onlookers clapped . . . and Hoagy vanished. The next act was due.

Doctor Terminus's eyes roamed over the crowd. They looked less hostile. 'I can't tell you how gratifying it is to hear beautiful music coming from that diseased throat,' he told them all. 'That's what the medical business is all about . . . people helping people. You should all have coughs.'

'Doctor!'

The melancholy cry issued from a bent old man. The crowd parted to let him hobble forward on his crutches. 'Doctor . . . Doctor . . . a miracle is all I ask!'

Hoagy's latest disguise fooled the people yet again.

Doc Terminus raised dark, expressive eyebrows and his blue eyes twinkled. 'He only wants a miracle,' he said, playing to his bewitched audience. 'How can I refuse him? If he's willing to pay for it . . . he'll get it!'

'Name your price!' cried the man boldly, indicating that no price was too high for a miracle.

Terminus held up one finger and Hoagy willingly handed over a dollar. In exchange he received a bottle of medicine. Hoagy unscrewed the cap, held the bottle aloft for dramatic effect . . . then drank the entire contents. For a moment nothing happened. Then, Hoagy appeared to be racked by convulsions. He staggered, and moaning, fell to the ground, rolling and twitching violently.

As with one voice the crowd murmured, 'Ah . . .!'

Seconds later, Hoagy was on his feet, the crutches flung aside. His movements, slow at first became faster and faster. He uttered a shout of joy and started to dance. He paused momentarily to look up at the doctor, tears of joy trickling down his cheeks. Then he danced again with an even greater display of vigour.

The trick had worked. The gullible crowd, obviously moved by what really appeared to be a miraculous cure, were filled with awe. The doctor was almost forgiven for past misdeeds.

A timid, middle-aged woman said defensively, 'I . . . I believe in the Doc.'

Another man added emphatically, 'I trust him!'

Hoagy stopped dancing long enough to clasp his hands together and say with firm conviction, 'I put my *life* in his hands.'

The doctor had done it again. The crowds were putty in his

hands. A moving forest of feet pushed eagerly round the stage, anxious to purchase his wonder drugs. Yes . . . today would be good for business. Debonair, spruce and brimming with confidence, he sang:

> 'My friends, you've seen a miracle –
> And you'll see many more.
> People will come pouring in
> From Land and sea.
> We'll have centres for testing;
> Let's start investing!
> Keep those dimes and dollars mounting;
> I'll collect and do the counting.
> Anyone who lives here will be
> Strong and healthy
> You'll be getting richer by the day.'

The townspeople echoed heartily,

> 'Yea!'

The doctor smiled. Now, he could afford to smile!

> 'Hear them acclaim us –
> This town will be famous.
> The whole wide world will look at us and *say* . . .'

The people knew what was coming:

> 'Poddo-ma-quassy . . . Paquo-ma-soddy . . .
> Passa-ma-massy . . . Quoda-ma-poddy . . .
> Passa-ma-daddy . . . Quoda-ma-passy . . .'

Hysteria mounted; everyone was confused now as they all shouted:

> 'Quodda-maddy . . . Dama-Daddy . . .
> Dappo-mossy . . . Quoda-Possy . . .
> Passa-Boddy . . . Passa-quassa-ahhh!'

Collectively, the townspeople cried,

> 'Passa-ma-*quoddy*!'

The doctor's grin was ecstatic. Good relationship had been reestablished, a victory achieved. For the present at least, he and Hoagy were safe . . . even welcome in the sleepy fishing village of Passamaquoddy. His eyes flashed and sparkled at the pretty girls as he sold his lotions, pills and medicines to the eager, clamouring crowds.

The magic jingle of coins was music to his ears. He was solvent again!

Chapter Five

In the lighthouse, Pete was proudly parading around in his new clothes. He had never owned anything new before and he was elated. The suit Nora had bought for him was light grey, complimenting the blue and white checked shirt and black bow tie. His eyes sparkled as brightly as his shiny new shoes.

Nora and Lampie were polishing the lens. Nora always liked everything inside the lighthouse spic and span. She never forgot the responsibility that she and her father had to keep all approaching ships aware of the dangerous rocks off the New England coast.

Lampie paused to admire his handiwork. 'Beautiful, beautiful, lens,' he remarked admiringly. 'It could send out a beam from the light of my pipe.'

Nora nodded and turned to Pete. 'Pete, if you'll just carry the oil up, we'll be ready for the night.'

'Sure,' he replied. 'After that, I'd like to show Elliott my new suit. He'll never recognise me.'

Lampie looked up, his face registering alarm. 'Wait, wait, wait!' he instructed. 'Don't bring Elliott up here. Government Regulation Number 302 says: Dragons are not permitted on the premises of a United States Lighthouse. Now fetch the oil so's I can enter in the log that you did it.'

Anxious to please, Pete murmured, 'Okay!'

He paused in front of Paul's picture in its handsome frame. After eyeing it for a few moments he asked, 'Nora . . . could I please take Paul's picture down to Elliott? Then he can start looking for Paul.'

The request was an odd one, and Nora was reluctant to let the picture out of her sight – especially into the hands of a little boy who was playing make-believe. Pete, sensing her doubts, looked disappointed, so finally she gave in.

'All right. Be careful with it. It's the only one I have.'

Delighted, Pete picked up the picture and ran down the twisting stairway.

When his footsteps had died away, Nora turned to her father with a grateful smile. 'Thanks, Dad,' she said softly.

'For what?' Lampie appeared to be surprised.

'For making believe about the dragon and going along with it. Means a lot to Pete . . . sort of a family he made up.'

A shadow flickered across Lampie's face and he pulled at the stubbly growth on his chin. 'Who's making believe? I saw that

thing with my own eyes. I'll never be the same again.' He fixed his daughter with a firm stare. 'If you haven't seen it, go down to the cave and your eyes will pop!'

Nora's fine brows drew together in a straight line. 'I was there. I saw nothing. Dad . . .' she pleaded, 'be realistic.'

Lampie met his daughter's warm brown eyes. 'You want to talk about realistic? Okay, let's talk how realistic you are . . . waitin' for someone to come back who ain't gonna come back.'

Lampie's reference to Paul was too much for Nora and she quickly averted her face, her expression withdrawn and sad.

Her father immediately regretted his harsh, thoughtless words and he spoke in a softer tone. 'Nora, I know how you feel. But if a year's waitin' hasn't told you nothin', then you're not the one to talk realistic, are you!'

It was a statement of fact to which Nora had no reply. She gazed unseeingly across the expanse of restless sea.

'Sorry, Nora.' Lampie crossed the room to place his hand affectionately on his daughter's arm. Suddenly, he was anxious to escape the anguish in his daughter's eyes. 'I . . . er . . . got to go into town . . . hardware store . . .' he mumbled.

He hurried away on his fictitious errand, leaving Nora all alone. Sighing softly, she walked out onto the narrow gallery which ran all round the top of the lighthouse. She gripped the railings and knew she was walking an emotional tightrope. Dusk had fallen early and purple clouds shot through with amethyst and ruby hung low on the horizon. Far below, the choppy seas crashed with unrelenting fury onto the dark, jagged rocks. The wind caught and ruffled Nora's coppery curls, and the memories flooded back.

As the lamp behind her flashed across the treacherous waters, her eyes misted. In a strong, sweet voice she started to sing of her love:

> 'I'll be your candle on the water;
> My love for you will always burn.
> I know you're lost and drifting,
> But the clouds are lifting.
> Don't give up – you have somewhere to turn!
>
> I'll be your candle on the water,
> Till every wave is warm and right.
> My soul is there beside you;
> Let this candle guide you;
> Soon you'll see a golden stream of light.
>
> A cold and friendless tide has found you.
> Don't let the stormy darkness pull you down.

56

I'll paint a ray of hope around you,
Circling in the air,
Lighted by a prayer!

I'll be your candle on the water;
This flame inside of me will grow.
Keep holding on, you'll make it.
Here's my hand, so take it.
Look for me, reaching out to show,
As sure as rivers flow,
I'll never let you go.
I'll never let you go . . .
I'll never let you go!'

Directly Pete left the lighthouse he hurried along the sandy beach to the cave where he had left Elliott the previous night. Bubbling with excitement, he was looking forward to seeing his dragon and telling him how kind Nora was. Reaching the black, yawning cavern he rushed inside, afraid that Elliott would no longer be there. But Elliott was very much in evidence, warming his tail over a fire made out of logs washed in by the sea.

The dragon was pleased to see him and grunted musically. Pete grinned and pivoted around for Elliott to inspect his new clothes. He raised one foot in the air.

'I've got new shoes, too,' he exclaimed happily. 'Look at the way they shine! Nora is so nice to me. I wish I could do something for her.'

Elliott blinked and nodded down at his little friend, his dragon eyes expressing devotion.

A wave broke noisily just outside the cave and white, spewing foam crept inside, forming small puddles. Pete remembered Nora's warning about the sea and said, 'I'd better go now, before the tide gets too high!' From beneath his arm he took the photograph of Paul and held it close to Elliott. 'Now . . . I want you to concentrate on finding Paul. This is what he looks like. Remember his face. Try real hard, will you?' he pleaded.

The dragon studied the face of the seaman in a peaked cap then nodding wisely, made a soft musical sound of agreement.

Pete beckoned to Elliott who bent down. Tenderly, Pete kissed the dragon's cheek. 'I have to go now,' he explained, 'but I'll see you tomorrow.'

Elliott semaphored a wave and Pete hurried from the cave, dodging between the shallow pools of water to protect his shiny new shoes.

Elliott, left once more to his own devices, concentrated very hard on Paul's face.

As the day had progressed, Doc Terminus and Hoagy had become steadily richer at the villagers' expense. Now they had found their way to the tavern beside the harbour. Drinks were bought for the doctor and in a benevolent frame of mind he condescended to examine the ears, eyes, noses and throats of the customers in the bar. Advising them in his medical capacity was, of course, highly profitable, as his supplies of medicines, tonics and potions progressively diminished. The doctor was attentive and sympathetic, smiling his attractive, wayward smile, and lining his pockets at the same time. He adjusted his silk cravat held in place with a diamond horseshoe pin, flicked an imaginary speck of dust from his elegant jacket and smoothed his moustache. He was well satisfied. Since this morning there had been a decided improvement in his relationship with the townsfolk of Passamaquoddy!

Hoagy, unable to hold his liquor very well, was showing signs of strain. Pushing his straw hat to the back of his head he complained, 'I'm gettin' tired of tryin' to explain why we got a sail on our wagon instead of horses.' To his befuddled brain, it seemed that every second person asked that same question.

Terminus smiled at another customer then hissed an aside to Hoagy: 'Would you rather tell them how we gave the horses away in Mattawanakeag to settle a malpractice suit?'

The memory of that unpleasant incident immediately restrained Hoagy. 'Nope!' he uttered lamely.

'Don't worry,' soothed the doctor, examining his immaculate white gloves with the airs of a dandy. 'When we leave this town we'll have horses again . . . and plenty more.'

'More what?' demanded Hoagy flatly, and hiccupped.

'More everything . . . more anything . . . I don't know. Do you mind if I sound optimistic?' The doctor lowered his voice to a confidential whisper. 'This is the worst town on our route. I hate Pas . . . Pas . . . Pastafazuli, or whatever the name is. I don't want to cure anybody here. They all deserve to have whatever they have.' He broke off to wave a friendly, enthusiastic greeting to a newcomer at the bar, then continued savagely, 'I've had nothing but bad luck here.'

The doctor's eyebrows arched in exasperation. The lighthouse keeper was weaving an uncertain path towards the table where he and Hoagy were seated. Lampie looked very drunk . . . and very determined, like a man who had something on his mind.

'See what I mean?' muttered the doctor in tones of extreme disgust.

Lampie swayed and stopped in front of the doctor. 'I'm sorry . . . so sorry . . . forgive me, Doc . . . Hoagy. Let me buy a round.' He signalled the bartender then leant across the table to whisper hoarsely, 'Doc, I gotta to talk to you about . . .' his voice slurred, dropped to a whisper, 'about somethin'!'

'Ah, an emergency case,' exclaimed Doc Terminus, reluctantly playing along. 'Sit down.'

The bartender arrived with a fresh supply of drinks and the three men toasted each other's health. The preliminaries over, Lampie leaned forward confidentially. 'Doc . . . you're a man of science . . .'

Flattered, the doctor gracefully accepted the compliment. 'A man of science . . . yes . . . I am . . . with degrees from the Royal Medical College in London; the Gleitzen Einen Peitzen in Vienna; and the Moulin Rouge in Paris. Why do you think they call me Doc? Because they sail their boats into me?'

He laughed at his little joke, but Lampie, very much in earnest, ignored it.

'Know anythin' about dragons?' asked the lighthouse keeper.

The doctor treated the question with contempt . . . the wild ravings of a drunken man. 'Of course I do,' he answered flippantly. 'I see them in all the big cities going down the street with that funny little walk, wearing bright colours, fluttering their eyes . . .'

'No, no, no . . . I'm talkin' about dragons . . .' insisted Lampie. 'Creatures that breathe fire, have claws and horns and wings, and . . . and . . .'

Doc Terminus humoured Lampie. After all, he had bought a drink. 'You want a veterinarian. Why do you ask?'

'Because . . . I saw one!'

The doctor was fast running out of patience. 'Is it sitting at the next table?' he asked sarcastically.

Lampie's face flushed. 'I saw it yesterday in the street. Belongs to a kid, name of Pete.'

'You're trying to tell me that there is a dragon here, in Passimacracker?'

'Yes!' insisted Lampie.

In an aside to Hoagy the doctor muttered, 'I told you this was a rotten town.' He turned back to Lampie. 'In my professional opinion, I think you've been up in your lighthouse too long.'

Lampie felt a sense of outrage. Wasn't anyone ever going to believe him? 'What if it's true? What then?' he demanded.

The Doc considered the question. 'Well, in my educated opinion, the existence of a dragon would have an impact of gigantic

59

proportions. Mythology and legend would become history and science. One could really make a buck with it.'

'I can prove it,' shouted Lampie, becoming very excited. 'Elliott . . . I mean . . . the dragon is in a cave down below the lighthouse. See for yourself!'

The doctor frankly thought the entire story a myth . . . the figment of a drunken man's imagination. Casually, he said: 'Unfortunately, I can't make it right now. I have an appointment with a young lady who's interested in a nursing career.'

Hoagy, in his drunken state was more than willing to accept the challenge. He cried hoarsely, 'I wanna see it!'

'Let's go!' said Lampie quickly, fearing Hoagy might change his mind. 'But first . . . we better have a quick one. Lotta rocks to climb. And that dragon is scary.'

Hoagy grinned stupidly. 'Let's have one for the rocks.'

Lampie raised his glass. 'And . . . one for the scary.'

The two men downed their drinks, borrowed a lamp from the bar, and staggered out into the night.

Doc Terminus watched them go, a cynical smile on his face. Dragons indeed!

The beach was dark and unfriendly, the surging sea licking at their feet but the two men sang as they dodged the waves. The beams from the lighthouse winked at them as they clambered uncertainly over slippery rocks and at last, more by accident than design, found the entrance to Elliott's cave. Hoagy took a bottle from his jacket pocket, raised it to his lips, then passed it over to Lampie. Their courage was wavering. They took their first few steps inside the eerie cavern and from somewhere deep in its interior came a strange, soft, even sound. Almost like someone snoring . . . with a difference.

Hoagy grabbed Lampie's arm and Lampie's voice shook. 'He's in there all right. Convinced?'

'I . . . I think so,' muttered Hoagy weakly.

'Then . . . let's get outa here!' Lampie's courage was fast disappearing.

'I wanna pet him!' insisted Hoagy, too intoxicated to fully realise what he was saying.

Lampie giggled. 'You must be crazy . . . 'cause I know you're not drunk!' He flung one arm round Hoagy's shoulders. Staying close together the men ventured right inside the cave, slowly inching forward, Lampie holding the light above his head.

'Remember . . . no matter what you s-see . . . stay c-calm . . .' warned Lampie in a shaky stage whisper.

Hoagy's eyes widened in sudden fear. 'What do you m-mean . . . n-no matter what I s-s-see?'

60

Elliott had been taking a nap but the sound of voices alerted him. Quietly, he moved behind a rock where he could observe – without being seen.

'Might as well g-give it to you st-straight . . . we're gonna s-see a h-hideous m-monster.' The lighthouse keeper's teeth chattered like castanets.

'Oh . . . no . . .' Hoagy wished now that he hadn't started out on the adventure. Why should he spend valuable drinking time deep inside a cave searching for a fiery dragon? His instincts told him to run – fast!

Lampie was still speaking. 'It's big . . . fifty feet of terror . . . claws so sharp they could t-tear a man to sh-shreds. Evil eyes that l-look right th-through ya . . . a tail, so powerful it could smash the hull of a frigate . . . wipe out a whole crew in one great sweep . . . a face horrible enough to turn a man to stone . . . a hero into a coward . . .'

Elliott had been pulling a sour face at Lampie's description of him. Now, he looked positively scared, too. Did he really look that bad?

Trembling all over, Hoagy placed a hand on Lampie's shoulder. Softly, Elliott crept up behind the two men, listening to Lampie's description. 'A flame that could roast you like a t-t-turkey . . . and a fearsome mouth that could chew you up and spit you twenty leagues . . .'

The monstrous, exaggerated description was too much . . . even for Elliott. The dragon placed a nervous claw on Hoagy's shoulder and the three of them moved forward at snail's pace. Hoagy, fortunately unaware of the dragon's presence, felt less nervous as the minutes ticked away. Then, suddenly, a movement behind him jerked him to a halt. He peered over his shoulder . . . and froze in horror.

'What's the matter?' asked Lampie.

Hoagy's mouth was twitching but not a sound passed his lips. Lampie turned to stare at his friend. Hoagy appeared to have shrivelled and he was jerking his thumb over his shoulder.

'It's g-g-g-got m-m-me,' he finally managed to stammer.

Lampie stared upward – straight into Elliott's big eyes. The lighthouse keeper screamed, a high pitched wail of sheer terror: 'Yaaaa . . .'

Hoagy screeched – and leapt right into Lampie's arms, almost bowling them both to the ground.

Poor Elliott shrugged. He could not understand what all the fuss was about. In an attempt to be friendly he made his soft, sing-song noise in an effort to say hello.

The two men stared at the dragon, their mouths hanging open.

Hoagy pinched Lampie's arm. 'Them eyes . . . I . . . lookin' right through us . . .'

'N-never show a d-dragon you f-fear him. Stop sh-shakin', and t-try to sm-smile,' advised Lampie, obviously terrified himself.

Hoagy was quaking in his shoes. 'Can't s-stop sh-shakin', and I . . . I'm smilin'.' His lips curved back from his teeth – a gesture entirely lacking in merriment.

Lampie made a desperate effort to pull himself together. 'Ah . . . hello . . . er . . . Elliott,' he ventured timidly.

Elliott made a friendly, but garbled sounding reply which made Lampie jump. 'See that, how smart he is?' he said to Hoagy. 'He's sayin' hello back to me. Now you gotta do somethin' that'll make him like you!' Lampie had a sneaking feeling that Elliott did like him . . . at least a teeny bit.

Hoagy wondered feebly what he could do to put himself on good terms with the huge dragon. Ah yes . . . the whisky! Taking the bottle from his pocket he removed the cork.

'Care for a belt, Elliott?'

Elliott was curious. He lowered his head until it was level with Hoagy's face. Shakily, Hoagy poured a generous amount of the liquor into the dragon's mouth. Elliott swilled it around, tasting it like a connoisseur, and licked his lips. Lampie and Hoagy exchanged glances, congratulating themselves on the move.

Their rejoicing was short-lived. Elliott suddenly realised that the whisky tasted awful. He tried to spit it out but the powerful fluid ignited his burners. At first, there was a harmless shower of sparks issuing from his nostrils, then with a loud roar, long flames belched forth licking the air, threatening to scorch the two men. They didn't wait around to see what was going to happen next. Slithering, sliding, falling over each other, they raced from the cave, crazy with fear.

Hoagy scrambled over cliffs and jagged points of rock, moving like the wind for the comparative safety of the village. Lampie headed for the lighthouse.

At the cave's entrance, poor disillusioned Elliott stood panting – his tongue hanging out to cool off in the night air:

When Lampie returned, Pete was sleeping soundly in his bunk, blissfully unaware of the incident which had just taken place inside the cave. On duty at the top of the lighthouse, Nora heard her father's faltering steps on the twisting stairs. As he reached the top, the reek of his breath announced that he had found his way to the tavern again.

Lampie leaned against the rail breathing hard, his eyes staring and glazed. 'Elliott . . . tried . . . to . . . roast us . . .' he gasped.

Nora struggled to be patient. 'Dad . . . please . . . don't start!'

Lampie appeared not to have heard her. 'Me and Hoagy were just standin' there. I said, "Hello, Elliott." He said, "Hello." He seemed to like me, you know? I mean, I could tell from his tone. Then he spit a flame at us!'

Nora was not in a mood to indulge her father's fantasies but she asked, 'What made him do that?'

'Hoagy gave Elliott a drink!' announced Lampie dramatically.

Nora managed a small smile. 'Well, there it is. Elliott doesn't drink with strangers.'

Lampie ignored the jibe. 'He got so mad. All those flames!' He staggered back against the rail and rubbed his bleary eyes. 'Better get a few hours sleep before my watch.' He glanced across at Pete, whose eyes were tight shut, a contented smile hovering about his lips. Lampie shrugged, commenting, 'Don't know how he can stand such an ugly beast!' Having delivered this final retort he shuffled uncertainly down the stairs to his bunk.

Nora leaned over the rails watching her father's descent. This frequent occurrence of dragon stories was highly disturbing. There couldn't really be a dragon . . . could there?

Chapter Six

Shortly after Hoagy and Lampie left the tavern in search of Elliott, Doc Terminus returned to his quarters. Brisk business had reduced his best selling line – a sea-water remedy. Now, he was engaged in making a fresh batch.

He stroked his beard thoughtfully trying to recall the exact quantities he had used the last time. 'Is it two parts fish oil, three parts sea-water, and six parts potato squeezings?' he mused. 'Or is it only two parts sea-water?'

The door suddenly opened and Hoagy burst into the room and leaned weakly against the wall. His clothes were soaked and water raced in tiny rivulets down his face. The Doc, busy mustering the ingredients for his unpalatable concoction did not look round. Hoagy tried to speak but not a word passed his lips. Shaking, he held out his hands in a gesture of appeal.

The doctor was still wrestling with his mental arithmetic. He looked up, counted six of Hoagy's fingers held aloft and jumped to the wrong conclusion. 'Six parts sea water? That much?' Nonchalantly he added more liquid to the brew. 'No wonder they love it,' he chuckled.

Poor Hoagy, trying vainly to divert the doctor's attention finally managed to stammer, 'S-s-saw it . . .'

'Saw what?' asked Terminus stirring the potion and at the same time wrinkling his nose at its unpleasant odour.

'Ell-Ell-Ell-dra-dra-'

The doctor's patience was sorely tried. 'What is an Ell-Ell-Ell-dra-dra-dra?' he asked scornfully.

Hoagy swallowed, took a deep breath and blurted out loud and clear, 'Dragon! I saw the dragon! Lampie wasn't lyin'! It belched flame at me.'

A note of hysteria in his assistant's voice finally attracted the doctor's full attention. Pausing to wipe his hands on his blue and white striped apron he frowned, saying, 'Belched? You saw a belching dragon?' His tone echoed disbelief. 'Sure you weren't belching yourself in front of a mirror?'

Hoagy emphatically shook his head. 'Never seen anythin' so horrible in my life! Thought I was a goner!' He rolled his eyes reliving those final moments deep inside the cave. 'There was no need for him to do that,' he muttered reproachfully. 'I only offered him a sociable drink.'

Terminus was exasperated. 'Hoagy . . . I can't have a drunk working for me.'

Hoagy lurched further into the room and gripped the lapels of the doctor's jacket. 'Doc . . . look at me! I'm not drunk. What I saw tonight sobered me in a second. I swear . . . I swear to you . . . there's a big, horrible dragon up in that cave. I swear!'

Terminus firmly removed Hoagy's hands from his clothes. His assistant's jabbering was idiotic. He dug into his pocket, brought forth a coin and tossed it. 'I just realised I can't stand you when you're sober. Get out of here and get yourself a good stiff drink.'

Hoagy was offended and hurt. He tried to protest but the doctor would have none of it. He had work to do and was determined that Hoagy's wild stories were not going to hold up production. Firmly pushing Hoagy towards the door, he shoved him outside, then recommenced bottling the sea-water tonic. By the morning he would have enough of it to float a ship!

The next day, Pete woke early, scrubbed his face until it glowed, brushed his hair and put on his smart new clothes. When he was ready, he and Nora walked into the village. It was a fine morning and the sun shone gold across the dusty streets and a layer of mist clung to the low lying hills.

On any other occasion, Pete would have been fired with enthusiasm at the prospect of an outing in Nora's company. But not today. Nora was taking him to school. Pete, uncomfortable and fidgety, watched the other children out of the corner of his eye. They ran, skipped, rode bicycles or walked, swinging their neatly strapped lesson books. None of them looked ill at ease.

Pete tried to impress Nora with his knowledge, hoping to influence her decision. 'Nine and nine are eighteen!' he said hopefully.

Nora smiled. 'Really?'

'Nine times nine are eighty-one!' continued Pete glancing up at Nora.

'Amazing!' she remarked.

Pete tried again. 'Two thousand pounds make a ton.'

'Wow!'

Pete pointed to the road sign. 'That says: Passamaquoddy.'

Nora remained adamant. 'You still have to go to school,' she stated.

Moodily, Pete kicked a stone. 'Do I have to like it?'

'Like it or hate it, you've got to go,' insisted Nora, her voice firm but kind. 'Do you want to be stupid when you grow up, like the Gogans?'

Mention of that dreaded name brought an immediate reaction. 'Okay, I like it, I like it,' agreed Pete.

Two of the village girls named Alice and Betty fell in step alongside Pete. At first they giggled and stared until Alice plucked up sufficient courage to ask, 'Are you the boy with the dragon?'

'Yup!' replied Pete briefly.

'Is it a he-dragon or a she-dragon?' enquired Betty shyly.

Pete sniffed contemptuously. 'You don't name girls Elliott.'

'Where is he?' demanded Alice.

Pete glanced over his shoulder. Sure enough, Elliott was trailing behind, visible to Pete . . . invisible to others. 'Following me,' he said casually.

Alice and Betty turned round, squinting into the sun. They couldn't see any sign of a dragon and as two boys from their class overtook them, Betty said, 'Elliott the dragon is walking right there.' She indicated a spot.

Eddie and George exchanged glances and tried to look impressed.

'I can't make out his colour,' said Eddie.

'Mostly green,' replied Pete, quite offhand.

'He's not too big, is he?' enquired George, laughing behind his hand.

'He's regular dragon size,' returned Pete.

By now, Nora and the school-children had drawn level with the quay, where a group of fishermen were airing their grievances, their voices loud, their faces red with anger. One of them pointed to his almost empty cart.

'I ain't got nothing to sell.' he complained lustily.

One of the fishermen knocked the ash from his pipe on his boot. 'So, I pulled my nets in, and there warn't a fish in 'em,' he moaned and shook his head at the injustice in the world.

'I just docked,' cut in another man. 'Ain't nothin' out in that ocean but water.'

The man with the pipe muttered. 'It's real strange, I'm tellin' you. It's like every fish sorta disappeared. Just suddenly up and disappeared.'

'Strange,' said the bearded man.

'Strange!' echoed the others. 'Strange and peeeculiar . . .'

Nora quickened her pace as the men growled and muttered darkly amongst themselves, but one of them moved away from the group. Tough and muscular in a short-sleeved shirt open at the neck, he glowered, pointing at Pete. 'There's the cause of it,' he accused. 'That kid!'

Nora swung round at the remark, frowning. The children clustered about her.

The man continued darkly, 'From the day he came to town, the fishin' went sour.'

Pete's face turned bright pink as Nora said stiffly, 'Don't be ridiculous!'

'It's that crazy dragon-talk of his,' cut in one of the other men, closing in.

The group were menacing. 'That kid's been nothin' but bad luck wherever he goes!' rumbled a fisherman with one lock of dark hair hanging insolently over his forehead.

Nora stood her ground, annoyance flashing on her piquant face. 'You're a bunch of superstitious ding-dongs!' she told them. 'You know that fishing grounds shift from time to time.'

Pete looked at his defender in admiration. She looked so fresh and pretty in her long white dress, a yellow bow holding her long, curly hair in place.

'Elliott will make the fish come back,' promised Pete.

'There he goes, talkin' dragons again!' snapped the man with the half-empty cart.

The tough, aggressive looking man in shirt sleeves tapped Pete on the shoulder. 'Hey, kid . . . there ain't no room in this town for a dragon. And there ain't no room in this town for jinxes like you neither!'

A shadow crossed Pete's face and he lowered his eyes to hide his hurt.

Nora flared. 'If there's enough room for a chowderhead like you, then there's more than enough room for a dragon.' She beckoned the children close, glared at all the men and sang:

> 'There's room for everyone in this world,
> If everyone makes some room.
> Won't you move over and share the world,
> Everyone make some room.
>
> Even a dragon deserves a place,
> A wide open space with no reigns, no chains.
> He wants to play games, to dance with you.
> Give him a chance to sing his song,
> He only wants to belong!'

Pete sang a refrain:

> 'There's room for everyone in this world,
> Will everyone make some room.
> Spread out while Elliott gets uncurled,
> Fly on his back – and *zoom*!'

Nora joined in:

'Rock him and ride him, and line up beside him.
You'll see how quickly you blend.
A dragon is just one more stranger
In search of a friend!

From an ant to a bird, to an elephant herd,
Let them walk, and fly, and roam.
Step aside, let them live, it's simple to give.
Like us, they just need a home!'

The school children chorused:

'There's room for everyone in this world.'

Nora agreed:

'Back up and make some room.
Let's all move over and share this world,
Everyone make some room.

Just think how far out the ocean goes.
The whirling wind blows shore to shore, door to door.
Think of the valleys and mountaintops.
The earth never stops.'

The children took up the melody again:

'So deep, so high, with miles of sky,
We all have part of the *pie*!
Welcome the dragon while you have a chance,
Give him his moment to rise up and dance!'

The children ran to the village green and danced, their warm
gusts of laughter ringing out beneath blue skies. Some of them
clambered onto seesaws and swings, scaled ropes and played tag.
School was forgotten. They were having fun.

Nora watched them, still singing in her rich, sweet voice:

'There's room for everyone in this world,
Will everyone make some room.
Love given freely can spare this world,
Let friendly feelings bloom!

Just give an inch, give a yard, never flinch,
When the time comes to offer a hand.
So let's all make sure

We give everyone somewhere to *stand*.
Let's all make sure
We give everyone somewhere to stand.
Just the way God planned it,
Just the way God planned!'

The sonorous, insistent clanging of the school bell brought the fun and games to an abrupt end. The children reluctantly turned their faces towards the schoolhouse. They had a strict teacher who objected to any pupil being late, no matter what the reason.

Miss Lorintha Taylor, the village school mistress was standing on the schoolhouse steps, her back stiff and straight as a ramrod, her face indignant. A prissy spinster, she was a stickler for discipline and already the children were flaunting their disobedience in her face. She pointed accusingly as they rushed inside the school, hoping to escape her eagle eye.

'LATE . . . LATE . . . LATE . . .' she stormed as a stream of pupils milled past. She grabbed Eddie by the ear.

'Ow . . .' The boy squirmed miserably in her spiteful grasp.

'Why are all of you late?' Miss Taylor demanded.

Eddie wriggled like an eel. 'We were playing with Nora and Pete and his dragon,' yelped the boy.

Miss Taylor's brows drew together. 'His wagon?' she queried. 'That's no excuse for being late. Get inside.' She released Eddie's ear, and scowling, he hastily joined the rest of the children.

Miss Taylor glanced along the street to make sure there were not any stragglers. Nora approached her, Pete at her side.

Nora smiled sweetly. 'Good morning, Miss Taylor.'

The teacher's attitude was clearly hostile. 'Good morning,' she replied icily. 'Thank you for making my students late and disrupting the entire schedule.'

Nora, determined to be pleasant for the sake of Pete's education, ignored the barbs and said brightly, 'You have a new student.'

Miss Taylor pointedly looked everywhere except at the boy standing at Nora's side.

'This is Pete,' remarked Nora, pushing him right under the teacher's nose.

'Oh . . . that!' She slid Pete a look of frank disapproval. 'Hmmm . . . if he's a transfer I'll have to have his records.'

Nora's excuse was swift. 'Unfortunately, his old school burned down and his records were destroyed.' She smiled encouragingly at Pete. 'Pete, give her nine times nine.'

'Eighty-one,' replied Pete briskly.

Miss Taylor's smile was thin and rather sour. 'Then I've got to have his birth certificate.' She rocked on her heels, certain she had won on this point.

Nora was ready. 'Tragically . . . the flames from the schoolhouse also set fire to the City Hall and his birth certificate went up with it.' She touched Pete's arm. 'Give her a ton.'

Obligingly, Pete said, 'Two thousand pounds.'

'Do you want him to spell Passamaquoddy?' enquired Nora.

Miss Taylor refused to yield. She was frankly unwilling to accept Pete as a new pupil. 'No, no, no!' she said haughtily. 'This is irregular! Irregular!'

'But he needs an education,' answered Nora tartly. 'You can't disagree with that!'

The two women's eyes locked in battle. Finally Miss Taylor capitulated. She had lost! 'I would . . . if I could,' she murmured stonily. Grudgingly, she stood aside and admitted Pete into the classroom.

Pete's reluctance to join the school matched Miss Taylor's reluctance to accept him. On the steps, the two women exchanged false smiles, then Nora made her way back to the lighthouse.

Pete was eventually allotted a desk and the first lesson of the day began. Beneath Miss Taylor's scrutiny the children bent their heads industriously over their books. For a while there was quiet; no other sound was heard but the occasional rustle of a page being turned, or a pencil scratching on paper. Then quite unexpectedly the solemn tranquillity was broken. The school bell began to ring. Everyone glanced up, looking curiously towards the window. The bell rope was moving; the bell was clanging . . . but who was pulling it? There was no-one near it.

Miss Taylor eyed her pupils suspiciously. 'Why is the bell ringing?' she snapped. 'No-one's out there!'

Had Pete been able to foresee the catastrophe his next words and actions would cause, he might have chosen to remain silent. He knew that Elliott was ringing the bell . . . Elliott, bored, lonely, wanting Pete to play with him.

Pete darted from behind his desk. 'I'll stop it!' he cried and rushed from the classroom. Miss Taylor followed, her lips pursed in a thin, disapproving line.

Pete grabbed the bell rope and held it tightly. 'Elliott! Stop it!' he ordered. 'The bell isn't supposed to ring till the lesson ends.'

Elliott wasn't concerned with the school's schedule. He enjoyed seeing the children at play. Jerking the rope he continued pulling . . . the bell kept on ringing. Miss Taylor in the background could see Pete wrestling with the rope and naturally concluded he was the culprit now. How the bell had tolled earlier no longer concerned her.

72

'Stop that! Stop that!' she ordered in a tone that brooked no good for Pete.

'I'm not doing it,' he protested.

'Liar . . . liar! It's the knuckle-cracker for you. Three for lying . . . and three for whom the bell tolls.' Roughly, she grabbed Pete by the scruff of the neck and dragged him back inside the classroom.

With a certain air of satisfaction she picked up a thin birch switch, a cruel smile playing round her lips. 'Hold out your hands – palms down, knuckles up!'

Poor Pete swallowed and did as he was told.

Miss Taylor brought the cane down. 'One . . . two . . . three . . .'

From the doorway a low agonised sound of protest told Pete that Elliott was watching. 'It doesn't hurt much, Elliott. It's not your fault she doesn't understand,' he cried.

Miss Taylor scowled. 'Who are you talking to?' She brought the cane down again. 'Four . . .' Pete winced but didn't murmur.

The teacher glanced up sharply. 'I'm talking to Elliott,' murmured Pete.

'Whom?' The cane swished through the air twice more. 'Five . . . six!'

'My dragon!' said Pete bravely.

'Dragon . . . wagon . . . nothing but a network of lies,' screeched Miss Taylor. 'Three more for your imagination. Seven . . . eight . . . and a great big nine!'

From beyond the classroom a growling sound deepened into a frustrated roar. Elliott wanted revenge. He watched . . . and waited!

Pete's eyes were downcast, his knuckles red and very sore. 'If this is school . . .' he thought.

'Stand in the corner,' snapped the teacher, her face smug.

Fetching a tall dunce's cap from a cupboard she placed it on Pete's head. Embarrassed and humiliated, an angry flush stained his cheeks. The children at their desks could barely repress their giggles.

'Back to work . . . *everyone*!' commanded Miss Taylor. The pupils knew better than to disobey and bent their heads over their books. Satisfied that she had the situation under control she walked towards her chair, her eagle eye on her pupils. Slowly, the chair was inched sideways by an invisible claw.

'Elliott . . . no!' Pete's plea came too late. Miss Taylor sat down and the chair was snatched away. Uttering a high-pitched shriek, she crashed to the floor.

Pete ran forward and righted the chair. From the dusty floor, Miss Taylor glared, her face black as a thundercloud. Loss of dignity in front of the class was not to be tolerated.

'You . . .' she blustered, 'you pulled the chair out from under me!'

Pete struggled to explain. 'Elliott . . . he didn't mean it! I mean, he did it . . . but . . .'

The teacher was back on her feet. 'That does it,' she exploded. 'You've had a taste of the knuckle-cracker . . . now . . . you'll have a dose of the behind-breaker!' She snatched a much larger switch, her eyes cold pinpoints of hate.

Elliott had seen enough. Intent on revenge he roared – a ferocious, deafening bellow – then he charged right through the school wall. It caved inwards and an enormous jagged hole was visible, shaped like a dragon. Chaos ensued. In the mêlée, children shouted and screamed in terror, desks were overturned, papers floated upwards. Mesmerised, shocked into stillness, Miss Taylor watched, the switch still in her hand.

Elliott wasn't finished yet. Picking a path through the debris, he wrenched the cane from the teacher's hand, breaking it into pieces, and pushed her roughly against the blackboard. She screamed, aware of a presence yet seeing nothing.

Pete intervened. 'No . . . no . . . Elliott . . . get out! Elliott . . . you're going about it the wrong way. Go back to the cave! Go on!'

Elliott was reluctant, but made a soft, sympathetic sound telling Pete how he loved and cared about him. Then he made a dramatic exit crashing through the wall at the opposite end of the room.

'I'm sorry . . .!' apologised Pete to the white-faced teacher and he, too, ran through the huge hole . . . away from the shambles: the direct result of his first morning in school.

The rest of the children followed Pete out into the sunshine. Miss Taylor, in a state of shock traced with her eyes the two distinct outlines of a dragon. Inelegantly, she slid to the floor! Miss Taylor had fainted.

Chapter Seven

Doc Terminus and Hoagy were in their quarters, the Doc attempting to repair the damaged skeleton. 'Why do I hear a bell ringing?' he asked, looking up from his grisly task.

'School must be out!' Hoagy peered through the window. Crowds of laughing children raced along the street, pointed excitedly at the schoolhouse, yelping like excited puppies.

'It's too early, stupid!' muttered Terminus, affectionately patting the skeleton. He joined his assistant.

'See? I told you school was out!' muttered Hoagy, pleased that for once he could prove himself right. Fragments of conversation floated on the morning air. 'Dragon! Elliott . . . Pete . . . dragon!'

The two men exchanged startled looks and the next moment, Terminus was outside the door and had intercepted a small boy.

'Ah tell me; what's going on?'

Breathless, excited, filled with a sense of importance, the boy gasped, 'Pete's dragon . . . wrecked up the school!' He ran off to join his friends and spread the news.

Hoagy's face was aglow. 'I told you . . . I told you!' he said.

The doctor's expression was a mixture of fascination and disbelief. He had to find out. Wordlessly, he rushed in the direction of the school. A large crowd had gathered and were gaping with bewildered faces at the huge dragon-shaped holes in the school walls. A man was carrying Miss Taylor to a chair on the street. Her skin was the colour of chalk and she was moaning . . . small, anguished sounds of terror. Someone produced smelling salts and thrust them under the teacher's nostrils. The crowd waited, expectant!

The doctor did not waste time on preliminaries but climbed in through one of the gaps to survey the wreckage. By nature a cynical man, even he was impressed.

Outside, Miss Taylor tried to pull herself together. Hysteria was unseemly for a lady. '. . . and the dragon . . . came through one wall . . . went out the other wall . . . without bothering to knock!'

Tongues wagged as villagers who normally despised the haughty school-mistress lent a sympathetic ear.

Hoagy enjoyed his moment of triumph. 'Now . . . do you believe me?' he asked the doctor.

Terminus made no reply but took his assistant by the arm and led him away from the scene of dereliction. The doctor had a strange look on his face . . . a calculating gleam in his blue eyes.

Much later, when the long shadows of approaching night were turning the air cold, the Doctor and Hoagy were seated inside their wagon. Terminus poured absorbedly over a dusty old volume. Suddenly, his face lit up. At last, he had found what he was looking for. He ran his index finger over the yellowed page, tracing the outlines of a dragon. Hoagy watched with less enthusiasm. The study of dragons was not his choice of topic.

Terminus asked suddenly, 'You think this kid, Pete, would sell it?'

Hoagy pushed his straw hat to the back of his head. 'Money talks!'

Terminus said, 'First there's a dragon. Now you tell me money talks. Will miracles never cease?' His expression was reflective. 'This dragon . . . is it in good condition?'

'Very good . . . too good,' replied Hoagy with conviction. Hadn't the dragon tried to burn him to a crisp just last night? 'A cream puff!' he added.

'How old would you say it is?' persisted the doctor.

Hoagy shrugged. 'I don't know how to tell a dragon's age! But . . . he had whiskers, if that means anything.'

'Whiskers . . . whiskers . . . interesting!' The doctor scanned the volume. 'It says here:

> "Dragon whiskers, dragon toes,
> A dragon tooth and a dragon nose!
> Every little piece, every little piece!
> We can make a million
> By slicing him, dicing him.
> Hoagy, we can sell,
> Every little shell.
> There's enough of him to go around,
> Money, money, money by the pound!
>
> Every little piece, every little piece!
> I can take my scissors
> And clip him up, rip him up.
> Every little part
> Is a work of art.
> Think of what a dragon heart would bring,
> Wrapped up in a ribbon and a string.
>
> Dragon liver can cure a cold,
> Dragon powder grows hair,

78

With dragon blood you never get old:
Every item is covered with gold!

Every little piece, every little piece!
Dragon, you're my wagon
To destiny, you're the key.
Every little shred,
Moving me ahead,
Every dream of mine will be fulfilled.
What a dragon business we can build!

Dragon cartilage keeps you thin,
Dragon fat is for burns,
A dragon tear will clear up your skin,
Watch the profits come rolling in!

Every little piece, every little crease!
Lead me to the dragon:
We'll buy him up, tie him up
Drag him from that cave,
Show him that we're brave!"

Hoagy's eyes rolled in horror.

'No, boss, no, you go yourself!'

Terminus ignored the comment:

We'll bind him up, grind him up,
Lop him up, chop him up.
Can't you hear that jingle-jangle sound?
It's money, money, money by the pound!'

The doctor slammed the book shut and a cloud of dust blew off the pages, making him sneeze. Determination and excitement illuminated his face. He had a plan. Soon . . . he would put it into action.

On the following afternoon, Nora and Pete were painting the bottom of the lighthouse. Pete loved working with Nora and his eyes sparkled as he dipped his large brush into the whitewash. A light breeze ruffled his red hair and he had the look of a contented boy. All his life he had longed to be part of a loving family; always, he had been compelled to remain an outsider. Now, he was on the inside, wanted and welcome.

Nora glanced at him and smiled. Daubs of paint covered Pete's orange check shirt and his face was streaked with white. It didn't matter. He was surpremely happy. That did!

Nora gazed along the beach and was surprised to see two men approaching the lighthouse. She watched them, her eyes curious.

Doc Terminus drew level, and tipping his hat with a courtly gesture, gushed, 'Afternoon, Miss Nora. So this is where you live.' He stared up at the tall, impressive lighthouse. 'I certainly couldn't corner you there.' He laughed at his poor joke and poked Hoagy in the ribs. 'I tell you, you've gotta have a sense of humour these days.'

Nora raised her eyebrows but did not reply. She was suspicious, sensing trickery of some sort. What was the doctor after?

Doc Terminus turned his attention to Pete. 'And you must be Pete,' he observed, smiling and rubbing his hands.

'Yes, sir,' answered Pete smartly.

'I'm Doctor Terminus and this is Hoagy, who's doing his internship with me.' He paused. 'I heard about that incident at school and . . .'

'I'd rather not discuss it,' intervened Nora swiftly.

Terminus made a good pretence of being sympathetic. 'I realise you must be disturbed about it, and up to here with dragons.' He touched his forehead before turning back to Pete with a syrupy smile.

'You know, Pete,' he said confidentially. 'I've always loved dragons. They're such wonderful creatures . . . when they're not busy destroying things, of course. I've had a dream since I was your age that one day I would have my very own dragon.' He clasped his hands together in a dramatic gesture. 'I would consider my life to be fulfilled – I would be *most* grateful if you'd sell me your dragon!'

There . . . it was out!

Hoagy flinched and swallowed nervously.

Nora could only express astonishment. 'You . . . want . . . to buy . . . Elliott?'

'Sight unseen . . . as is!' retorted the doctor promptly.

'We'll give him a good home,' added Hoagy for full measure.

Pete listened to the wash of the waves swishing tirelessly on the beach and thought of dear, faithful Elliott hiding in the cave. 'I couldn't sell him,' he stated firmly.

'Sure you could,' coaxed Terminus. 'That's what life's all about . . . buying and selling. Give you three dollars,' he offered.

Hoagy whispered furtively, 'Offer 'im four!'

In an aside, Terminus croaked, 'I'll offer him five. It'll make his head swim.'

Smiling, looking the part of a benevolent benefactor he said to Pete, 'Five dollars!'

Pete blinked. 'I can't sell him. I don't own him.'

'What do you do . . . rent him?' joked Hoagy.

The doctor's patience was limited. 'Who owns him?' he demanded.

'Nobody, I guess. He just came to me.' Pete explained, 'He only goes to those who need him.'

'I need him,' breathed the doctor, his voice hoarse.

Nora frowned. There *was* something decidedly suspicious about the doctor's offer. 'Doc, I don't know what you're up to, but you'd better forget about this. He's not for sale.'

The doctor's polite attitude dissolved. 'Nora, go shine your brass,' he snapped rudely.

Trying to win Peter over, he lowered his voice and took the boy's arm. 'Pete, my boy . . . you're conversant with Elliott. Talk to him . . . tell him how much I need him. Deliver Elliott to me and the money is yours . . . plus a bottle of my medicine that's guaranteed to bring on puberty two years ahead of time! That's better than a dragon!'

A challenging smile tilted Nora's lovely mouth. 'Doc . . . maybe you should talk to Elliott yourself,' she suggested.

'Where is he? Does he speak English?' retorted the Doc boldly.

'He's down the beach.' Pete led the two men to the cliff edge and pointed.

Terminus and Hoagy peered along the sand, but no matter how hard they looked, they could not see any sign of a dragon.

'Where?' demanded Terminus shortly.

'Right there . . . by the water,' said Pete, smiling. Elliott was clearly visible to him . . . but not to anyone else. The dragon was playing at the water's edge, jumping over the frothing waves as they crashed onto the shore.

The Doc and Hoagy, clearly frustrated and confused, exchanged glances. 'I still don't . . .' began the doctor.

Pete understood. 'That's because Elliott's invisible today.'

Nora had joined the trio and now she and Pete burst into helpless laughter as they examined the faces of the men. They were still chuckling as they raced back to the lighthouse.

'The kid's a con artist,' raved the doctor. 'Almost took me for a fiver and a bottle of goop.' His fury increased when he looked over his shoulder and heard fresh peals of merriment. 'They know they're sitting on a gold mine. Well, they had their chance to make a few dollars.'

They turned to go back the way they had come. Mission defeated, at least for the present. 'That dragon doesn't belong to anyone,' grumbled Terminus. 'He's fair game . . . and he's gonna be ours:

> We'll bind him up, grind him up,
> Lop him up, chop him up.
> Can't you hear that jingle-jangle sound?
> It's money, money, money by the pound!'

Hoagy chuckled but the next moment, both men leapt several feet into the air. Nora and Pete, watching from the lighthouse, rocked with mirth. They had deliberately sounded the foghorn as the men passed by. That should teach them a lesson in manners.

Lampie, asleep in his bunk, woke up with a start. Jolting into an upright position he rubbed his eyes, bounced out of bed like a rubber ball and ran to find Nora. She and Pete had returned to their whitewashing.

'The fog! Where's the fog?' blurted Lampie, blinking in the strong sunlight.

'There's no fog,' explained Nora, her face still creased with laughter. 'We were just using the horn to chase a few buzzards.'

'Oh!' Nonplussed, Lampie scratched his head then turned to survey the job in hand. Pete was slopping whitewash sideways. The result was messy and streaked. 'Got an early start, I see,' said Lampie.

Nora stepped back a pace and nudged her father and they watched Pete trying to come to grips with the work. Lampie grinned and picked up a brush. He worked on the wall with vertical, even strokes. 'You got a real masterpiece goin' there, Pete,' he observed. 'Only . . . what is it?'

Nora's eyes sparkled. She looked at her father and said, 'Why, anyone can clearly see it's a picture of you.'

Lampie paused to stroke his stubbly white chin and ask, 'I look that good?' He resumed his brush work. 'Look here, Pete. Up and down, up and down. That's the way to whitewash.'

Pete nodded and energetically copied Lampie's strokes. He quickly got the idea. 'This is fun,' he laughed.

Lampie dropped his brush into the pail. 'If you like it so much, I'll just go and take a little nap while you finish up yourself.'

Nora grabbed his arm, pretending to pull him back and make him do more and Pete, watching them, felt a surge of happiness. Being with Nora and Lampie was fun . . . really fun. 'This is the best time I've ever had in my whole life,' he told them both.

Nora and Lampie exchanged swift glances, a secret message passed between them. Lampie nodded.

Nora said softly, 'Pete, Lampie and I have talked it over and we feel that the time has come for you to stop running. If it's all right with you, we'd like you to live here with us.'

Pete swallowed, so overwhelmed that for one dreadful moment he thought he might cry. Instead, he took a deep breath. 'Oh . . . Nora . . . Lampie . . . do you mean this could be my real home?'

Nora nodded.

'And Elliott too?'

Lampie was on the point of raising an objection. Sensing this, Nora hastily intervened. 'Sure. And Elliott, too!'

'But he has to sleep in the cave,' added Lampie. He had no intention of letting a huge green dragon with pink hair and breathing fire sleep inside the lighthouse. Not even for Pete.

Pete's face was radiant. 'Oh, yes . . . yes . . . thank you . . . thank you . . .' He flung his arms around Nora, hugging and kissing her. She ruffled his silky red hair, her own heart filled with gratitude for the small, dynamic boy who had entered her life and brought love and laughter with him.

Lampie was next. Pete hugged him, too, forgetting that he was still holding his paintbrush. 'Hey, not on me! On the lighthouse!' insisted Lampie laughing good-humouredly as he rubbed the whitewash from his face.

Pete grinned, dipped his brush into the bucket and tackled the lighthouse wall. 'Okay . . . up and down . . . up and down . . .'

When the job was finished, Nora, Lampie and Pete hauled themselves on a pulley to the top of the lighthouse. They cleaned the windows, rubbed the lens and polished the brass until it shone. While they worked, they sang:

'It's a brazzle dazzle day,
So throw off the past and everything in it.
That's the brazzle dazzle way –
Enjoying your time from minute to minute,
Running through the sand without your shoes on,
Making sure that you don't keep your blues on,
Finding a boat we can cruise on.

It's a brazzle dazzle day
When you think of love and never of sorrow.
That's the brazzle dazzle way –
To do your work now, and take off tomorrow.
Flying through the air you don't need wings on,
Climb right up and feel the thrill it brings on,
Rock with the wind as it sings on!
Ride higher and higher, and glide above the clouds
free –

No-one to catch us or slow us,
Even the birds are below us!

It's a brazzle dazzle day,
A lifetime of joy in just a few hours.
All our brazzle dazzle years
Have just begun, we'll follow the sun,
And replay this brazzle dazzle day!
This brazzle dazzle day!

When your job becomes a frolic,
You've become a brass-aholic!
All our brazzle dazzle years
Have just begun, we'll follow the sun,
And replay this brazzle dazzle day!
This brazzle dazzle day!'

Their chores all finished, Pete stood at the rail of the lighthouse and gazed out over the ocean. A fresh southerly wind blew off the water, puffs of creamy foam broke onto the beach. In the distance he could see the harbour and the brightly painted little boats beneath a wide blue shawl of sky. He was bursting with excitement, curiously tinged with relief. At last . . . at long last, he had a home.

Chapter Eight

A dirty, ramshackle cart drawn by a pair of scrawny horses clattered down the winding hillside road which led to the village of Passamaquoddy. Wearing sour, hawk-like expressions, the unkempt Gogan family searched the faces of every passer-by. They were hoping for a clue . . . any clue which might lead to the recapture of Pete. Since the loss of the boy they had treated no better than a slave, life on their ill-run farm had gone from bad to worse.

Lena Gogan was in a particularly foul mood. She pursed her lips, refusing to believe that Pete, without money or friends, could simply vanish. Just wait till she caught up with him. She would quickly teach him the folly of his action. She clutched at a grubby blue document for reassurance. Yes . . . Pete was hers by law. She had the adoption papers to prove it.

The wagon rattled along the high street until Merle Gogan shouted at the horses to stop. They whinnied and pulled up opposite Doc Terminus's medical cart.

The villagers stared curiously at the unwashed strangers dressed in tattered clothing, and gave them a wide berth. Grover and Willie stared back, wearing insolent grins. At a given signal they roared together, 'Dragon!'

The word brought instant fear to people's faces. The Gogans were delighted. Now, they were convinced that they were on the right track.

'This is the place, all right,' grunted Merle Gogan. Snapping the reigns he urged the horses forward and the wagon moved off down the street.

Doc Terminus was engaged in treating a luckless patient suffering from toothache. The terrified man's mouth was filled with an assortment of dangerous looking mechanical contrivances. Rivetted to the chair, his haunted eyes expressed sheer terror.

Terminus smiled reassurance and prepared to plunge a claw-like instrument into his patient's mouth. Just at that moment, Hoagy dashed into the tiny enclosure, spluttering with excitement. He whispered urgently in the doctor's ear.

Terminus frowned. 'It would be unethical of me to leave my patient at a time like this.'

'It's important . . . about the dragon!'

The words had an instantaneous effect upon the doctor. The

patient and his toothache were brushed aside. 'Be right back, sir,' he explained briefly, any brace of ethics forgotten. 'Stay tense. Don't relax or that clamp will break your jaw, tear your gums apart and go clean through your cheek!'

The shattered man sat immobile in frozen horror, not daring to move a muscle.

Terminus joined Hoagy on the street and Hoagy pointed. 'See that wagonload of worms? They're lookin' for the kid and the dragon!'

The doctor stared at the back of the dirty wagon and its four shabby occupants. 'I knew there'd be competition,' he fumed, convinced that the Gogans, too, wanted the dragon for themselves.

Unaware of the dark cloud hovering on his horizon, Pete was enjoying life that afternoon. Nora and Lampie had taken him out on a dory and he wriggled happily, rocking the small craft. Sunlight glinted on the water, sea-birds darted overhead, and Pete's chest swelled with pride as he helped haul in a lobster pot.

Nora clapped her hands in delight. 'One dinner coming up!'

'I got one! I got one!' yelled Pete excitedly.

'Reach in there and pick him up,' advised Lampie, his eyes twinkling.

'I'm afraid to,' admitted Pete. 'You do it.'

Lampie grinned and shook his head. 'Who . . . me? I'm a lighthouse keeper, not a lobsterman.'

'I'll do it,' volunteered Nora and edged over to the lobster pot. Reaching inside, she grasped the wriggling, clawing creature and held it aloft. In the afternoon light it had a muddy tinge and looked ugly and unappetising.

'Well, well, well . . . if it ain't our own little lost runaway orphant!'

Lena Gogan's hateful voice booming over from the nearby wharf instilled first shock, then fear into Pete. He sat rigid in the boat staring across at Lena's face, as muddy and unappetising as the lobster he had just caught. The dreaded moment he had lived through in his nightmares had arrived. They had found him! He wanted to hide . . . run . . . anything to escape the vile family perched like vultures on the pilings along the wharf. Instinctivey, he turned to Nora for protection.

'The Gogans . . .' he gasped.

Nora's face registered astonishment and dismay. Pete had often talked of the family and mentally she had visualised slovenly people. But these creatures . . . she shuddered with revulsion.

Never . . . *never* would she release Pete to such unscrupulous morons. She would defend him in any way she could.

Lena grimaced showing the gap at the front of her mouth. 'You look nice and clean. Guess all them good manners I taught paid off.'

Grover was leering at Nora. 'Who's the pretty lady, li'l brother?'

'Yeah . . . innerdoose us,' bellowed Willie in his coarse voice.

Pete, frozen in despair sat with bowed head. The bottom had just dropped out of his world.

Nora took the initiative and boldly tackled the situation. She stood up in the tiny craft and Lampie followed suit. He pulled Pete to his feet and the trio faced the evil Gogans. Nora called across the expanse of water, 'I'm Nora. Pete is staying with me.'

Lena Gogan's discontented mouth snapped shut and she heaved her fleshy body into an upright position. 'She's tryin' to break up our happy family. Go get 'im, boys!' Her pedestal of chins shook with anger.

Merle, Grover and Willie needed no urging and grabbed the ropes swinging over the side of the wharf, lowering themselves into a dinghy. They were determined the brat would not slip from their grasp this time. Lena tried to follow the others but not being agile, she plummeted onto the small boat like a sack of flour, nearly swamping them. For several moments, muttered oaths filled the air. Finally, the tangled sea of arms and legs was sorted out and the Gogans pulled away from the wharf, heading unsteadily towards the dory.

Pete, stunned by this twist of fate, pleaded, 'Please don't let them get me. Elliott went to look for Paul!'

Nora pressed him firmly down into a seat and reached for the oars. 'They won't get you,' she promised. 'Come on!'

'We can outrow those landlubbers,' shouted Lampie, as determined as his daughter to protect Pete. He leaned over to haul in the anchor. It would not budge. He tried again, his face red with effort as he strained and heaved. Beads of perspiration dripped from his forehead as he said tersely, 'Anchor won't come up. Must be snarled!'

Pete could not take his eyes from the Gogans. Their boat was only a few yards distant. The gap was rapidly closing and he watched, frantic with fear.

A splintering crash announced that the Gogans had arrived, ramming the dory. Scrambling to their feet, they attempted to board the tiny fishing vessel. Nora picked up an oar and swung it, holding the Gogans at bay.

Lena held out her hand. 'We'll jes' be takin' him back now, to his own home sweet home.'

Pete cringed.

Nora's eyes flashed. 'You won't be gaking him anywhere,' she announced sharply.

Merle Gogan snarled, his patience at an end. 'Okay, lady . . . move outa the way or we'll move you out. Right, boys?'

'Right, Pa,' said Grover his lecherous eyes fixed greedily on Nora. 'Willie, you grab Pete whiles I hold onto her.'

'You grab Pete,' replied his brother savagely. 'I wanna hold onto her.'

'I'll hold 'er!' yelled Grover.

'I'll hold 'er,' snapped Willie.

Fighting and shoving each other, they both tried to climb into the dory but almost fell into the water. Their father grabbed them by the hair and struck them viciously.

'I'll settle this. You two grab the brat. I'll do the holdin' of her!'

Lena jerked her hand on her husband's arm. 'Iffen you try to hold her like my boys wanna hold her, you'll be holdin' your head!' Plunging her hand inside the neck of her dirty dress she withdrew an equally grubby document . . . her Bill of Sale. She addressed Nora in impudent tones. 'Lady, he's ours. See this?' She brandished the paper, glared at Pete and sang in a cracked voice:

> 'We got a bill of sale right here
> That says he belongs to us.
> We bought him fair and square last year,
> And we own the little cuss.
> Look here. Read the writin'
> That gives us a legal claim.
> Oh, we got a bill of sale right here
> With dear little Pete's name!'

'Let me see that!' demanded Nora.
Lena hastily pulled the document away.

> 'We got a bill of sale in hand
> And lady, if you don't budge,
> We'll pick you up right where you stand,
> And bring you before the judge.'

'No, sir!' said Nora, her voice determined. She glared at the whole family and they all chorused back:

> 'That boy is our property,
> Same as the family cow!
> 'Cause we got a bill of sale right here
> And we're gonna take him now.'

Nora replied:

> 'You can't have him, you don't love him.
> All you've done up to now is break his heart.
> You'll abuse him, and just use him.
> Watch out or I'll take you apart!'

She stared up at the tallest of the two brothers, bravely facing him as he lunged towards her, while his mother screamed:

> 'But . . .
> We got a bill of sale right here
> He's ours until he dies!'

Pete listened to Lena's final words in a frenzy of despair. How could Nora fight the law? Was his destiny with the mean-spirited Gogans, after all? He wouldn't let them take him . . . he *wouldn't*!

As though in answer to Pete's anguish the waters suddenly parted following a mighty splash, spray showering in all directions. No-one realised what was happening – except Pete. Everyone was arguing, but Pete knew his prayers had been realised; Elliott had returned in time. Still invisible, he would soon make his presence felt.

'Elliott . . . help!' pleaded Pete looking at the waters in the harbour. His words were lost in the confusion.

As the Gogans surged towards the dory, Nora and Lampie strove to hold the menacing family at bay with their paddles. Nora chanted:

> 'Stay where you are! just one move more,
> And you'll get it between the eyes!
> You won't make a slave of him,
> Even if you connive.'

The Gogans mouthed:

> 'Yes we will, 'cause
> We got a bill of sale right here!
> We got a bill of sale right here!
> Petey's got to do his chores,
> Paint the barn and wash the doors,
> Shine shoes, turn screws,
> Fix a broken fuse.
> He's so good at feedin' hogs,
> Pitchin' hay and choppin' logs,
> We'd like to see you try it!'

Nora's temper was up. She replied:

> 'You can't have him, you don't love him.
> All you've done up to now is break his heart.
> You'll abuse him, and just use him.
> Look out or I'll take you apart!'

Lena sneered and the Gogans chorused together:

> 'We got a bill of sale right here
> That says he belongs to us.
> Fight all you want! won't do no good
> To holler and fume and fuss!'

Nora stamped her foot, her eyes flashing.

> 'Leave town, keep on going,
> Before I can count to five!'

Had it not been for Elliott's timely intervention at that point, there is no knowing what might have happened, but . . .

Suddenly, the invisible, torpedo-like dragon slammed viciously into the Gogans' boat with such force that it disintegrated on impact. The shattered planks flew apart, leaving the evil family struggling, bewildered, in the water. Spluttering, gasping for air, the half-drowned Gogans struck out for shore, Lena clinging determinedly to her sodden Bill of Sale. Spitting and clawing, they managed to haul themselves up onto the wharf. A moving forest of feet hastily retreated; none of the onlookers willing to leand a hand to the unsavoury farmer and his family.

No-one . . . except . . .

Help was closer to the Gogans than they realised.

Concealed behind a piling, Doc Terminus and Hoagy had watched the entire fiasco. The doctor smiled maliciously, his devious mind had already conceived a plan. It boded no good for Pete – or his dragon!

Chapter Nine

Unaware of Doc Terminus's scrutiny, the Gogans hurriedly left the wharf and headed for the local tavern. Once inside, they grouped themselves, shivering, around a table. The other occupants stared across the smoke-filled room at them, but kept their distance – the narrow windows looked out upon the harbour and the afternoon's events had not gone unnoticed.

Merle Gogan called for drinks, his voice as ill-tempered as his expression. Brandy was placed on the table and Lena seized hers greedily, her false teeth chattering against the rim of the glass.

Rapidly, the bar began to fill up, as news of the incident travelled. The local residents, sailors in dark blue jerseys and men with seamed, weather-beaten faces exchanged gossip over their pints, casting furtive glances in the direction of the Gogan family.

Doc Terminus and Hoagy easily traced the Gogans to the tavern but for a while, the doctor stood well back. His fastidious, almost fanatical concern for his own personal hygiene and smart appearance was deeply offended by the Gogan's apparent lack of cleanliness. Hoagy adjusted his tie and frowned, bristling disapproval, too.

With a certain reluctance, the doctor eventually moved forward. If his plan was to succeed he would require the co-operation of the uncouth group. As he approached their table he wrinkled his nose in sharp distaste; the Gogans smelled very unpleasant. Taking care to stay upwind, the doctor adopted a false air of camaraderie and beamed widely, blue eyes twinkling.

'Excuse me, folks. I witnessed what happened today, and I'm completely sympathetic with you.'

'What's sympathetic mean?' asked Grover, showing his ignorance.

His father kicked him viciously under the table and waited for the doctor to proceed. Before he had a chance to open his mouth, Lena said huskily, 'I think I got peeneumonia, Doc!'

'Sit here,' invited Merle tapping the seat beside him and fixing the doctor with his flinty eyes.

Doc Terminus gingerly sat down.

'Got this ache in my back . . .' continued Lena, determined to list her ailments.

Terminus ignored her and spoke to Merle, pretending respect.

'What's rightfully yours . . . is rightfully yours. You want Pete. Right?'

'Right,' echoed all the Gogans.

Terminus spoke slowly, distinctly. '*I* . . . want the dragon!'

The Gogans were stunned momentarily by this remark, then amused. Thinking the doctor quite mad they broke into wild, hilarious laughter.

The doctor's bushy eyebrows drew together in confusion. He misunderstood their merriment. 'Unless of course . . . *you* want it.'

The Gogan family could scarcely believe their ears. How utterly ridiculous to actually believe in the existence of a live dragon. They laughed even harder.

Lena complained, 'Now I got a pain in my side, Doc.'

Crafty Merle Gogan, however, had had a thought. If the fool thought there was a dragon, and was willing to help recapture Pete . . . well, it was worth listening to what he had to say. He motioned to his family to be quiet. 'You really want the dragon?' he asked.

'Very much!' replied Terminus with enthusiasm.

'What you willin' to give for it?'

Terminus had that answer ready. 'The help you need getting Pete. I'll need the same kind of help getting the dragon.'

Grover, Willie and Lena could not control their hysteria and fell about in their seats until Lena finally slid onto the floor. She sat up to rub a rapidly rising bump. 'Now I got a pain in my head, Doc.'

Pointedly, Terminus turned his back on the gross woman. 'Have we got a deal?' he asked Merle.

Merle paused, taking time to ponder, not willing to appear over eager. At last he shrugged. 'You might be of some help. Sure, why not!'

Doc Terminus was exultant, victory within his grasp. He stood up, whispered a few instructions to the scrawny farmer and said finally, 'Be ready at sunset!'

It was a deal. Merle's skinny, claw-like hand reached out, grabbing the doctor by the sleeve. 'Say Doc, whatcha gonna do with this . . . dragon?'

'Oh,' said the doctor breezily, 'maybe put him on a ranch, breed him . . . big stud fees.'

Even the Gogans could not fail to be impressed.

The doctor waved and moved rapidly out of range, Hoagy close behind. Outside, they both inhaled deeply, filling their lungs with fresh air – glad to be away from the unpleasant odour issuing from the Gogan family. Terminus smoothed the red silk band on his hat, placed it upon his head and hurried along the narrow street.

94

There was much work to be done if all was to be ready before sunset.

Close by, a group of discontented fishermen were seated round a table in the fish market. Their faces were gloomy and they muttered among themselves, pointing angrily to their empty baskets. When the Doctor and Hoagy approached, they looked up, expressions nakedly curious.

The doctor touched his hat to them. 'Ahoy, ahoy. How'd you like to make the fishing good again?'

It was a pertinent question; the men would like nothing better. 'How do we do that?' growled one man, his face brown as a nut from constant exposure to sun and sea.

'Catch the dragon, throw some nets over him and haul him away. Goodbye Elliott, hello fish!' The doctor made it sound relatively easy.

The fishermen exchanged glances, then nodded in total agreement. The Doc might just have the answer. Terminus outlined his plan then, smiling roguishly, hurried away.

The Gogan family arrived and all around the boathouse was a hive of activity as everyone worked with a will, making ready the huge nets to trap Elliott. Only one person stood idle. Lena Gogan leaned on a garbage can shouting encouragement, her voice shrill and cackling.

Nora, Lampie and Pete had hurried back to the lighthouse after the episode at the wharf, and now Pete was filling a lantern with oil. An urgent tapping on the window made him glance round and he was startled to see Elliott's nose pressed hard against the glass. He beckoned and Pete rushed to open the window, overjoyed to see his friend, anxious to thank him for his gallant effort earlier that afternoon.

'Oh, Elliott, you were terrific the way you saved us from the Gogans.' Pete's face shone with love and admiration.

Elliott nodded quickly, dismissing that subject and made a series of small, excited sounds.

Pete listened. He, too, became excited. He pushed a lock of hair from his eyes. 'You mean it?' he asked.

The dragon indicated that he certainly *did*.

'Wow! That's great! Wait'll I tell Nora,' breathed Pete, his cheeks flushed. Leaning right out of the window he gave Elliott a big kiss. 'You're the most wonderful dragon in the world,' he exclaimed. He could hardly wait to break Elliott's news to Nora. Giving the dragon a final hug he said goodnight, closed the window, and darted off to find Nora.

Elliott waved, then, smiling in the darkness, strutted proudly along the cliff.

Nora and Lampie were at the top of the lighthouse making preparations to set the beams in motion. Nora looked anxious as she gazed out of the window. Daylight was fading, the shadowy hills had turned purple and an angry red glow suffused the western sky. Way below, the restless waters churned and bubbled with the fury of a witch's cauldron and storm clouds swept low across the horizon. It was going to be a treacherous night. Just how treacherous, Nora had no way of knowing!

Suddenly Pete burst into the room, his face animated.

'Nora . . . Nora . . . good news! Elliott found Paul and he's on his way home.' The words tumbled over each other.

Nora swung round sharply, her face shadowed. 'Pete . . .'

Lampie looked solemn. 'You oughtn't to say things like that, Pete.'

'But it's true. Elliott said . . .'

'Please!' Nora held up her hand for silence. Then her face softened and she smiled gently at the boy. 'We've done enough talking about Paul – and about Elliott. It's time we were both . . . realistic.' She hesitated over that final word and looked across to her father. 'Paul's ship went down. He's not coming back and I've got to adjust my life to it.' She sighed. 'Pete, you've got to make a big adjustment, too. You have us now. You don't have to make believe your only friend is a dragon.'

'I'm not making believe.' Pete blinked back tears of disappointment.

'That's what I mean by realistic. There are no dragons,' said Nora.

'Except for Elliott!' Pete appealed to Nora's father. 'Lampie, you've seen him, haven't you?'

Lampie looked uncomfortable. 'Well . . . I coulda sworn I saw him, but you know . . .' He shrugged.

Pete's enthusiasm, his faith in Elliott was difficult to quench. 'Wait till Paul gets here. Then you'll know how realistic Elliott is.'

'Okay, Pete. Until that time, let's try not to talk about it.' She changed the subject. 'How about filling the reserve oil can?'

'Sure.' Pete picked up a bucket and tramped down the stairs, feeling deflated. Nora simply would not believe that Paul was alive . . . she didn't even believe there really was a dragon. Why were grown-ups so obstinate, he wondered.

Nora and Lampie watched Pete descending the stairs. When he was out of sight, Nora gripped the lighthouse rails, her voice

unsteady. 'Well . . . at least one of us is entitled to have illusions.'
Her eyes misted as she turned to watch the long, searching fingers
of light probe the ocean. Lampie, silent and sad for his daughter's
unhappiness over the missing Paul, touched her arm in a gesture
of sympathy, then slowly made his way to the kitchen. It was
obvious that Nora wished to be alone with her thoughts.

Softly, Nora started to sing the lovely song, 'I'll be your candle
on the water'. The tragic loss of Paul had affected her more deeply
than anyone could realise.

Night had fallen, bringing with it all the promise of a violent storm.
The wind was steadily rising and the waves roared, flinging heavy
white spray over the jagged rocks along the coast. The villagers
paid little heed to nature's violence as they scurried back and forth
from the old boathouse at the wharf, carrying ropes, canvas and
tackle. Doc Terminus supervised the activities, rubbing his hands
in satisfaction. A man with few assets but high hopes, he expected
soon to be a man of considerable wealth.

He called to a man balancing on a ladder, 'Put separate trip-
lines on the primary tarpaulin, on the secondary net, and on the
tertiary net!'

Merle Gogan's lips curled back in a sneer. 'The tertiary . . .'

'Doctor-talk,' remarked Lena.

The doctor wondered irritably why the men could not follow
simple instructions. 'Wait a minute, wait a minute! You've got it
all backwards.'

Hoagy sighed as he trailed a length of heavy netting along the
ground. 'We put the primary up first, then the secondary . . .'

Terminus disagreed. 'The primary has to come down first! That
means it has to go up third . . . and the tertiary goes up first!'

It sounded double-Dutch to Hoagy. He scratched his head.
'Then what about the secondary?'

Terminus tried to show tolerance. He did not find it easy. 'The
secondary is second! It's so simple! One-two-three! We're gonna
catch a dragon in this trap . . . not a guppy! It's got to be done
perfectly and with precision. Now follow me carefully . . .' Chant-
ing loudly so that his voice would carry above the screech of the
wind, he instructed:

> 'The first is the tertiary,
> The second is the secondary,
> The third is the primary net.
> The first is third,
> The second is second,

The third is the primary net,
Get it?'

Hoagy tilted his hat.

'Got it!
The first is the first,
The second is the first . . .'

Terminus was frustrated. He repeated his instructions loudly and prayed that at the vital moment, the men and the nets would not let him down.

'Can't you do anything right?' he asked Hoagy in exasperation. 'I've got to go get the kid. You rehearse this thing, and make it run like clockwork. Or else I'll have them chisel on your gravestone . . .'

With that threat ringing in his ears, Hoagy watched his boss walk away.

Inside the lighthouse, Nora trimmed the wick, then moved away from the rotating lens. Tonight, all men at sea would require the warning beams of light – and a prayer! She looked across the black expanse of water, tasting the tang of salt on her tongue. The premonitory roll of distant thunder, and a strange inner sense warned her that she must be constantly alert.

Pete clattered up the stairs carrying the spare bucket of oil always kept in readiness to refill lamps. Nora smiled at him warmly and took the bucket. Reflecting on what she had said earlier about being realistic she hoped she had not upset the boy. 'I'm sorry for the things I said.'

Pete grinned cheerfully and brushed a lock of hair from his forehead. 'I just didn't think the good news about . . .' he hesitated, 'you know . . . Paul . . . would make you feel so bad.'

Nora put her arms round his shoulders. 'I feel better now, and stronger, because you made me see the difference between wishing for things and facing facts. I appreciate that and I thank you for it.' She kissed his cheek.

'But Elliott *did* say . . .'

Nora cut off the sentence with an admonishing smile. 'Pete!'

'Okay, okay,' he muttered. For some reason, Nora would not face facts. 'I'd better get some wood for the stove,' he said and vanished again down the stairs. He reached the kitchen and found Lampie shaking coffee grounds from the pot.

The lighthouseman looked up, smiling guiltily. His conscience, too, had been giving him trouble. He put the pot onto the table and turned to Pete. 'Hey, Pete, listen. I shoulda backed you up about . . . you know . . . Elliott.' He blinked owlishly and stroked his whiskery chin.

'That's okay,' replied Pete, good-naturedly.

'No, it's not okay,' insisted Lampie. 'I saw him twice . . . I mean . . . I think I saw him twice. Only both times somebody must've slipped something into my . . . er . . . coffee. You know what I mean?'

Pete knew. Lampie meant he had been drinking each time at the tavern before running into Elliott. 'I know,' he responded.

Lampie said, 'I'm never sure of anything. Otherwise, I'd be out there skippering a ship like I wanted, instead of what I am – just some kind of lamp-lighter.' He looked dejected.

'You do important work,' defended Pete knowing that what he said was a fact.

Lampie had developed a true affection for the boy who had so recently entered Nora's life and his own. He touched his arm, saying, 'Right, right – that's me . . . important.' He shook his head, not convinced. In a tumble of words he suddenly said, 'Look, Pete, if you're sure of Elliott, stay sure, and don't let anybody shake you from what you believe. You got something going for you that nobody's got. Don't ever lose it.' He beamed and hugged Pete.

Pete swallowed hard, feeling that Lampie was allowing him to bridge the gap between boy and man. Wordlessly, he rushed outside into the teeth of the wind and headed for the woodpile . . . right into the arms of Doc Terminus.

Pete jumped in surprise.

The doctor was breathing heavily and looked upset. 'Pete . . . Pete! It's Elliott!'

The boy frowned, instantly worried. 'What's the matter?'

Terminus twitched his dark moustache. 'Elliott's in Passa . . . Packa . . . Dacka . . . He's in town! And he's tearing the place apart! You gotta do something!' He shook Pete. 'Come on!'

Pete was horrified. What could have happened to upset Elliott?

So well had the cunning doctor enacted his role that it didn't enter the boy's head even for a second, that this was a dastardly trick to woo him away from the lighthouse . . . and into a trap where the Gogans lay in wait.

Pete said, 'Come on,' and sprinted off to the village, Terminus at his side.

Nora, totally unaware of the drama taking place by the woodpile, checked the barometer, then picked up the telescope. Focussing it, she stepped out onto the narrow gallery running round the top of the lighthouse. The fierce wind cracked like a whip, tugging at her clothes, almost knocking her over. Far out to sea a ship was heading shorewards. For a while she watched it, fascinated, yet terrified for its safety. One moment it was visible, the next it had vanished as it plunged down into the waves. Had she known who was on that particular ship, her anxiety would have increased a hundredfold.

Aboard the vessel, the captain was shouting, 'We should be in the channel.' He narrowed his eyes against the spray and stared intently into the impenetrable gloom. He clung with the helmsman to the wheel, hanging on grimly, for tonight, in the rip-roaring gale, it seemed to have a mind of its own.

The helmsman gasped breathlessly, 'I hear breakers, Captain!'

A cabin door swung open and Paul emerged. Crossing the deck by means of a rope, he shouted, 'We should've made Passamaquoddy Light by now. It's my home port. Didn't think I'd ever see it again!' He tried to gaze through the darkness, hoping his fervent wishes would bring the fishing village into focus.

As the men shouted to each other their words were whipped away in the wind's fury. Waves rose upward, looming through the hurling spray. Would the ship stand up to the battering? Surely the shore was receding? The sombre canopy of night was rent aside as long fingers of light flashed out across the churning waters . . . the Passamaquoddy Lighthouse.

'It's a welcome sight,' muttered the captain.

Homesickness swept over Paul, and a wave of nostalgia. The lights beckoned . . . the lights of home. 'Looks great to me,' he shouted hoarsely. 'I know the lightkeepers – personally.' He smiled, visualising Nora's lovely face. His unexpected arrival would certainly come as a shock.

The captain swung hard on the wheel. 'Give me three points to starboard,' he cried, aware of the treacherous rocks looming ahead. Valiantly, the men faced the heavy seas together, comrades fighting for survival. They were aware of their extreme danger but as long as the lighthouse was there with its broad beams searching the ocean there was every hope they would not run aground, or worse, crash onto the waiting rocks.

Meanwhile, Pete and Terminus were racing along the beach in the direction of the old boathouse, heads lowered against the buffeting wind. Pete looked anxiously around as the wharf came into view. There wasn't any sign of Elliott. In fact, the place appeared to be deserted, and where was the violent upheaval the doctor had spoken of?

Pete stood still. 'Where's Elliott?' he demanded.

Coarse guffaws of laughter at his elbow made his blood run cold. There was only one such appalling sound in the whole world, and

he swung round in terror. It was a trick. His worst fears were realised as the Gogans pounced. He was their prisoner.

Lena pressed her dirty face close and leered, 'Yer phoney dragon's out helpin' Santa Claus pull his sled.'

Pete, desperate and scared half out of his wits tried to run. Willie kicked him, Grover cuffed him and Lena grabbed him by his hair, shaking him like a dog. 'You won't never git away agin!' she promised. 'Gonna put a chain on yer when yer workin', and when yer ain't workin' too.'

'Okay, okay. Flog him on your own time,' cut in the Doc. 'Right now, he's the bait for the trap. Take him over there.' He indicated the boathouse. 'Where that thing can see him when he comes through the doors.'

Pete wriggled and squirmed but against the entire Gogan family he didn't stand a chance, and was dragged away.

Terminus issued Hoagy with his instructions. 'He'll head straight for Pete. We'll spring the trap. After the tertiary net drops on him, I'll give you a signal and then you fire the harpoon right into the middle.'

Pete's anguished face expressed sheer horror. 'No! Nooooo!' he pleaded.

'Yes, yes!' replied the doctor, without a vestige of remorse. He turned to Hoagy. 'Got it?'

Hoagy nodded, looking more confident than he felt. At times, the Doc tended to confuse the issue. 'I got it. The only thing I don't know is how you're gonna get that monster . . . that hideous beast . . . that nightmare sent by the devil . . . to come here.'

'Easy. We send someone he knows to bring him here.'

Hoagy frowned. 'Who'd be crazy enough to do that?' He backed away, a suspicion suddenly forming in his mind.

'You!' smiled the doctor.

'Nooo. Oh, no,' pleaded Hoagy.

'He knows you . . . trusts you,' explained Terminus patiently.

Hoagy's laugh held a note of hysteria. 'It's a love-hate relationship.'

Terminus was fast losing patience. He wasn't going to have his carefully laid scheme sent awry because Hoagy felt squeamish. He grabbed his jacket and said in a threatening tone, 'You will go. You will bring him here. We're all on this earth for a purpose, and your purpose is to bring a dragon to a certain place at a certain time. This will fulfill you as a human being. Now, go!'

Shoving Hoagy fiercely in the direction of the beach, Terminus faced the villagers who had crept from their hiding places. He reminded them of the tertiary, secondary and primary nets and the fishermen nodded, their faces grim. The sooner the dragon was captured, the sooner the seas would provide an abundant harvest again.

Pete trembled as he watched the stage being set for the wicked deed. If only there was some way to warn poor old Elliott . . . but there was not. The Gogans had no intention of letting their prisoner escape.

Chapter Ten

In a daze of fear, Hoagy staggered along the beach barely able to keep his feet. The storm was at its height and progress was slow. The wind tore at his clothes and the small lamp he carried threatened to go out at any moment. A vivid flash of lightning illuminated the craggy rocks, shiny and black as jet. The shoreline looked unfamiliar – eerie and menacing. Thunder roared directly overhead and the dark sky suddenly ripped open. Hoagy was scourged by the rain as it lashed earthwards, sharp arrows of water driven before the merciless wind.

Trembling from a combination of cold and fear, Hoagy finally reached the cave where Elliott lived. His legs shook and he couldn't hold the lamp still.

In a muffled voice he called, 'El-el-li-ott-ott,' hoping against hope that there would not be a reply.

He listened. From inside the cave an odd sound floated towards him. Gingerly, he edged forward. In the thin stream of light from his lantern, Hoagy found the dragon – fast asleep.

Fear had frozen Hoagy's face into a mask. 'Oooooohh . . . Elllll-lioooot. Yooooohooooo . . .'

Elliott stretched – all twelve feet of him and opened one eye. Was Pete visiting him? In the dim light he saw Hoagy and remembered the fire water. He opened both eyes and wriggled his long tail with an air of menace.

'Easy, easy, fr-friend. I'm a friend!' stammered Hoagy praying that the dragon would believe him. Elliott stood up. 'Hon-honest. I g-got a mess-message about P-P-Pete!' Hoagy was ready to run. Why had he come on this wretched mission? 'Whoa, boy! Down!' He took a deep breath. 'The Go-Go-Gogans g-g-got Pete!'

There, it was out at last!

Elliott showed immediate signs of distress. He lumbered towards the exit and Hoagy, panic-stricken, ran . . . right into the cliff face. A shrill ringing began in his ears. He couldn't move. Snorting impatience, Elliott picked him up and rushed onto the beach, moving at speed, Hoagy clutched in his large claw. Hoagy, terrified, survival uppermost in his mind, gasped out where the dragon could find Pete. Elliott snorted, made himself invisible and flew towards the boathouse.

To an observer it would have appeared that Hoagy was flying unsupported through the icy air.

Half an hour after Pete had left the lighthouse to fetch wood, Nora descended the stairs to the kitchen. She longed for a cup of coffee and it was time for Lampie to take over the watch. She entered the cosy room and smiled at her father. Then she looked around for Pete. Puzzled, she asked, 'Dad . . . have you seen Pete? He was going for wood.'

Lampie shook his head. 'Haven't seen a hair of him. Or a stick of wood, for that matter.'

Nora felt threatened by unknown forces. 'There's a ship off the point, a nor'easter blowing up, and I can't find Pete anywhere.'

'Could be down the cave feeding Elliott leftover pie,' Lampie volunteered.

Ignoring her father's remark about the dragon she cried in alarm, 'The surf will flood the cave. Take the watch!' Pulling an oilskin off a peg near the door she plunged out into the night.

Groping her way along the cliff path, Nora was thankful for her familiarity with every twist and turn of this stretch of coast. Reaching the cave in the minimum of time she called, 'Pete! Pete!'

Her voice echoed back, an empty, hollow sound.

Cupping her hand to her mouth she called Pete's name again, then surprised herself by crying, 'Elliott!' In the darkness her face coloured in embarrassment. She had actually called to a dragon which she had convinced herself was non-existent. But she knew this was not the moment for analysis. Pete was not in the cave, and premonition warned her that he could be in grave danger. Below, in a darker level of her consciousness she sensed a threat to the red-haired boy she had come to love. She ran back along the beach, braving the onslaught of the battering wind and stinging rain. It was just possible that Pete had returned to the lighthouse during her absence.

Lampie had watched his daughter rush out into the night with a mild air of amusement. She was probably fussing about nothing. The boy would turn up. He climbed the stairs to start his watch. Not until he reached the very top did he realise the unspent fury of the storm. As he watched, the waves dashed against the rocks below with frightening force, and shot up against the side of the tower, breaking against the windows. Suddenly he felt apprehensive and as the wind gusted at near hurricane force he prayed that the huge panes of glass protecting the rotating lens would not shatter. He made a thorough check and breathed a sigh of relief. Everything was in order. His relief came too soon – problems lay ahead that even Lampie could not anticipate.

He swung round at a sharp sound behind him. Breaking glass!

Far below, the churning waters had spewed and spat out several large rocks with terrible fury. Flying upward, they struck the top windows of the lighthouse, smashing them. In the next instant, Lampie was knocked over by the sheer force and weight of thundering sea-water. He managed to stagger to his feet but another cloud of spray washed him halfway down the stairs. Dazed, he scrambled determinedly back to the top. His heart sank. The lantern house was black as pitch. He knew the wicks must be soaked. Wind and water surged in through the gaps. The position seemed hopeless, and he was alone. What had happened to Nora?

Not too far distant, the lone ship floundered in the raging seas. On deck, the helmsman knew a moment of panic. 'Captain! The light's gone!' he yelled.

'That's impossible!' The captain spoke sharply, unwilling to believe so dire a statement. Seconds later he knew it to be true.

For the first time, Paul was really worried. With the lighthouse to guide them he had never doubted they would make rough, but safe passage to the harbour. But now . . .

'There's a reef between us and the channel,' he warned.

All three men tried to penetrate the black wall ahead. There was nothing to be seen. No reassuring light; only inky blackness and the sound of screaming demons in the wind.

Nora, hurrying back along the beach was suddenly aware that something was wrong. She paused and looked ahead. The lights . . . the beam was out. But how? Shocked, she climbed the cliff face and sprinted as jagged lightning split the black sky.

Stumbling, falling, it seemed to take forever to reach the lighthouse. 'Dad . . . Dad . . .' she cried anxiously, racing up the stairs, almost choked with fear.

Lampie was standing at the top, his back to the wind trying vainly to relight the wicks.

Nora's face was pale, her nerves raw. 'Can you get it lighted?' she gasped.

'Gotta put dry wicks in,' said Lampie in a practical voice, fighting to keep calm.

Nora waited in a fever of impatience while he went for a fresh supply.

At the boathouse, Pete struggled frantically with the Gogan brothers – a vain effort which only brought him further blows.

The waiting fishermen tensed their muscles, ready for action.

It was about time that Hoagy returned.

Pete, in a frenzy of despair, cried out, 'Elliott! Elliott! Don't come in here. Stay out, Elliott!' He would have risked anything to save his friend, but he was held in a vice-like grip.

Lena Gogan snarled, 'I'm sick of hearing that name. Don't you never talk about dragons no more.'

Pete could have wept in frustration. His face was drained, white as paper in the dim light.

Hoagy, still held aloft, cried tremulously, 'Here comes the dragon.'

Doc Terminus was thrilled. This was the moment he had schemed for. 'The dragon! The dragon! Battle stations, everyone!' he ordered. 'He's coming in here. Haul up the primary, secondary and tertiary.'

Chaos reigned. Everyone rushed in different directions and the Gogans held Pete so tight he could scarcely move a muscle.

From his vantage point in the dragon's claw, Hoagy pointed. 'There he is, Elliott. See? I told you. Come on!' He wriggled to free himself. The dragon kept a tight hold as he charged forward.

The Gogan brothers passed Pete over to their parents and seized a trip-line in readiness. Hoagy, scared stiff, screamed at the top of his lungs, 'He's holding me. Holding me in his arms like a baby.'

No-one showed the slightest concern for Hoagy's dilemma.

'Look out, Elliott!' shrieked Pete. 'It's a trap!'

Elliott rushed into the boathouse. The waiting men were at a disadvantage. They couldn't see Elliott; they could only sense his presence.

'Doc . . . Doc! Get him now! He's right here!' Hoagy frantically waved his arms.

The Gogan brothers pulled the trip-line, a canvas tarpaulin dropped from the rafters, and poor Elliott was trapped. So was Hoagy.

'Help! Get me out! Help!' shouted Hoagy. 'Elliott, leave me alone. I'm just a victim like you.'

The unscrupulous doctor's eyes sparkled. 'Got him! Secondary net . . . go.' A heavy net fell, covering the tarpaulin. The final net fell, too, and beneath the masses of mesh, the shapes of Hoagy and Elliott were easily distinguishable as they heaved and struggled.

The Gogans stared in open-mouthed disbelief. 'Am I seein' what I think I'm seein'?' asked Merle.

'It's lookin' like a . . . it's like a . . .' Lena, blinking owlishly, could not bring herself to utter the word.

'Dragon!' snapped Pete.

'Don't say that,' echoed Lena and Merle together, suddenly scared.

'Elliott! Elliott!' wailed Pete. 'Over here!'

'Don't say that neither!' Lena clamped a dirty hand firmly over the struggling boy's mouth and hustled him towards the door.

They'd seen enough and wanted to be on their way before that dragon got loose.

It was Pete's final chance. His fight for survival. Once the Gogans took him away he would be a prisoner for ever. 'Elliott! Help! Elliott!' he screamed as he was dragged in the direction of the Gogan's wagon.

Elliott heard. Roaring in terrible anger he dragged the stakes, the nets, the tarpaulin and the clinging men along with him as he searched for Pete.

Hoagy, still in the tangled web with the dragon appealed for aid. 'Yaah! Doc! Help!'

The doctor groped beneath the surging mass of net and found Hoagy. 'Get out of there,' he snapped irritably. 'You're ruining the trap.'

Hoagy emerged, dishevelled and breathless. The Doc allowed him no time for slacking. 'Man the harpoon gun. Light the fuse.'

Seconds later, the fuse was sizzling ominously.

Pete looked back, saw what was happening and went beserk. 'No . . . no . . . don't shoot Elliott!' His voice was hoarse from shouting. Dear, lovable Elliott, still trapped under the netting, unable to see – he was a sitting target for the deadly harpoon gun. Pete sunk his strong, white teeth deep into Lena's hand. She screamed in pain, releasing her savage hold. Pete moved with the speed of a shot from a catapult, charged at the harpoon and knocked Hoagy to the ground.

The gun spun round in a semi-circle. The diversion had saved Elliott, for the moment at least. But the Gogans pounced on Pete.

The dragon shuffled ahead, still trying to sense Pete's presence. 'There he goes,' shouted Doc Terminus. 'Quick . . . get a bead on him!'

Pete was flung roughly onto the filthy floor of the wagon and Grover picked up an evil-smelling sack. 'Elliott! Help! Don't let them take me!' Pete's wail of misery brought an unexpected reaction.

Elliott materialised. Right in front of everyone . . . one huge, green, impressive and very angry dragon. No-one could move for the moment. They gaped, paralysed with fear. Belching flame, Elliott cast off the netting and moved in Pete's direction.

Terminus was the first to recover. 'He's getting away. Let's go after him,' he shouted. Victory was so close – he must not lose his valuable prize.

The Gogans had other worries. Elliott towered above Lena and Merle as they attempted to reach their wagon. Merle backed up, treading on Lena's foot. 'Yah! Don't bite us!' he entreated. 'You can have 'im back!'

Lena covered her eyes, too terrified to look at the green, belching fury. 'We don't never want 'im again,' she whimpered.

'Don't let 'im git us, Pa!' snivelled Grover who had tied Pete inside the sack and moved away from the wagon.

'Do somethin', Pa!' urged Willie.

'I'm doing something!' Merle ran away. His two sons followed.

Elliott spotted the squirming bundle in the back of the wagon. Growling with rage he picked it up and returned to glower down at Lena. She stood trembling, alone, deserted by husband and sons.

'I got a Bill of Sale . . .' she begun. Elliott's growl made her jump, flames licked close to her face. 'But I don't want it no more,' she shrilled and threw the crumpled document into the air. The dragon shot out a long, hot flame and the paper floated earthwards in tiny, charred pieces. Lena's Bill of Sale no longer existed!

Lena started running. She had never moved so fast in her life before. 'Hey, wait for me,' she yelled. Merle, Grover and Willie were on the wagon. She flung herself at the tailboard as the horses jumped skittishly and dashed off into the night. Cursing, Merle pulled her aboard.

Terminus, still determined to capture the elusive dragon was working on the gun with Hoagy. The doctor's foot caught in a coil of rope as his assistant shouted a warning. Too late! The gun fired . . . the rope knotted around the Doc's foot and he was jetted upwards with the harpoon. Right through the roof of the boathouse!

Pete was free from the smelly sack and as the gun fired, Elliott and Pete both looked round. Then they saw the doctor dangling high in the air behind the harpoon. The instrument had imbedded itself in a dock-crane and the doctor swung back and forth, back and forth, like a pendulum. Boy and dragon laughed heartily. It served Doc Terminus right!

Hoagy looked annoyed. 'You ruined my aim,' he accused the Doc.

'Got to do something!' muttered Terminus, not concerned with Hoagy's shot which misfired but with the wealth he would lose if he lost the dragon. 'The dragon'll get away,' he yelled from his swinging position.

Hoagy scratched his head. 'I know. I'll give him a bottle of your goop.'

'It'll only make him stronger,' said Terminus as he swung dizzily past again.

'It'll kill 'im,' retorted Hoagy flatly.

'How dare you! It's guaranteed to . . . Well, it's worth a try!'

Elliott had been listening and he moved over to the two men

who had hatched a vile plot against him, using Pete as the pawn. Rearing on his hind legs, he shook his pink hair and glared.

Hoagy felt his knees buckling. 'Oh, he's gonna eat us all up,' he wailed.

Terminus, at so desperate a moment, was still thinking of ways to line his pockets. 'Wait a minute, Elliott!' he said boldly, still swinging back and forth. 'I wanna make a deal with you – to buy up your used and spare parts . . . like a hangnail . . . or if you shed your skin . . . or if your hair falls out. I'll pay you top dollar . . .'

The dragon roared his fury – a low, rumbling sound like a volcano ready to erupt.

Hoagy had had enough. 'Let's get outa here!'

Terminus made one final bid. 'What's the matter with you, Elliott? Haven't you got any business sense?'

The dragon reached out with one claw and vigorously shook the harpoon rope. Terminus dropped to the ground like a stone. Shaken, he picked himself up and for once uncaring about the dust on his suit, he tore off after Hoagy.

They jumped onto their medical wagon. They had seen enough of the dragon . . . more than enough of Passamaquoddy!

'We ain't got no horses! How we gonna get outa here?' moaned Hoagy, his throat dry with fear.

'Hoist the sail. There's more than enough wind,' snapped Terminus, in a vile temper.

The wagon suddenly gathered speed. 'There, I told you,' said the Doc.

'But I didn't hoist the sail,' protested Hoagy, eyes wide with fear. He peered over his shoulder. Horror of horrors! Elliott was pushing them!

'Maybe he wants to come with us,' volunteered the Doc uncertainly.

'He's tryin' to get rid of us. Look out!' warned Hoagy.

Elliott was a smart dragon. He knew exactly where two scoundrels deserved to be. He catapulted Doc Terminus, Hoagy and their wagon right through the doors of the jail-house!

Chapter Eleven

Elliott's reputation was destined to change dramatically during that memorable and stormy night. From notorious menace he would rise to the dizzy heights of a public hero. Already, Pete had been saved from the Gogan's clutches, the artful doctor and Hoagy accelerated into the local jail. These two acts were to Elliott's credit. But there was more to come.

Pete was weary with the exertions of the night, and now he was anxious to return to the lighthouse. Nora would be worrying over him. He and Elliott made their way back through the village, the high-pitched whine of the tearing wind making speech almost impossible. An ominous creaking overhead caused Pete to look up and instantly, his eyes widened in alarm. A telegraph pole had split and was swaying dangerously, ready to fall. At that precise moment the main door of the Town Hall opened and the Mayor, accompanied by his councillors and Miss Taylor, emerged. Warily, the school-teacher stood back while the Mayor inspected the steps. His recent mishap when they had been suddenly whipped away was still fresh in his memory.

This particular night was not fated to be dull, either. The telegraph pole groaned loudly and instantly snapped in two. One half hurtled towards the small group huddling fearfully on the Town Hall steps.

Disaster seemed imminent!

'Elliott! Elliott! Save them!' screamed Pete.

The dragon responded. Reaching out a huge claw he caught the pole neatly as it fell mere inches from the Mayor and his cronies.

For a long moment there was a stunned silence, broken only by the boisterous wind. The Mayor was the first to recover.

'Elliott, the dragon!' He blinked in astonishment. There really was a dragon with pink hair and a long, lashing tail. The villagers were not, after all, suffering from mass hysteria. Right now the dragon did not look fierce, either. Yes, he was actually grinning down at him wearing a soppy, self-conscious expression.

Even Miss Taylor was impressed. 'He saved us,' she breathed and managed a thin smile.

The rest of the party were recovering from their initial shock. They were all anxious to press hearty thanks on the dragon and Elliott would have been forced to listen but . . .

A short, desperate, ear-splitting blast drowned out all other sounds. Automatically, everyone swung round to face the lighthouse. There was no mistaking that deep, clamorous din. It was the foghorn!

People muttered in agitation. The lighthouse was in darkness. What could have happened?

Pete did not waste time considering the calamity. There was an emergency. 'The light went out! Come on, Elliott!' he urged.

The dragon was still clutching one half of the telegraph plle. He dropped it nonchalantly into the gutter, hoisted Pete onto his back, spread his short, powerful wings and rose into the air. The crowd cheered, their voices faint, barely perceptible above the wind's lament.

Inside the lighthouse, Nora was in despair. Without a guiding light the ship in distress, crushed down among walls and valleys of inky water could run onto the rocks at any moment. Lampie's attempts to relight the wicks had proved futile. A constant deluge of rain and sea-water made the situation impossible.

Through the almost inpenetrable gloom, Elliott distinguished the lighthouse and flew down to land on the gallery at the top. Nora's back was towards Pete and his dragon, or she might have dropped her lantern in surprise.

'Come on, Elliott!' encouraged Pete, but when the dragon tried to squeeze inside, he was too large and the greater part of his bulk remained outside. Pete climbed in and dashed across to Lampie.

'What's the matter?' he asked breathlessly.

Lampie wrung his hands. 'Everything's wet . . . that's what's the matter!'

'Don't worry, Lampie. Elliott's here!'

Lampie rolled his eyes in disbelief. 'That's all I need now . . . a dragon in here,' he retorted irritably. His face grey with worry, he looked up at the lens – and jumped. Elliott was staring at it, too. The night had brought shock after shock. This was the greatest! The dragon could not be a mirage, not this time. Lampie was very, very sober.

Nora, unaware of the drama behind her, the roar of the sea, the scream of the wind blotting out everything, peered into the darkness. One moment, the swinging lamp was in her hand, the next moment, the gallery was awash with icy sea and spray, the lantern gone. Nora was knocked sideways, and she clutched at the rail for support.

'Dad! Hurry up!' she shrieked.

Spinning round, she almost fell into the churning waters below. There, mirrored in the huge lens was an even larger, bright green dragon. She shook herself. She was having an hallucination. She must have struck her head when the seas dashed her against the rails. She paused fractionally before hurrying inside the lantern house.

Nora gasped and hung onto her senses. This was no time to faint. Elliott was a fact – a very visible fact! 'Elliott! He's real! Really real!' Her eyes looked large as saucers.

Pete clutched Nora's hand. 'Of course he is. He's gonna light the wick.'

Eagerly, Nora asked, 'Can he do it?'

'Can he?' Pete's voice was full of pride. 'Why, he can throw a flame from here to Bar Harbour. That is . . . if he can get his own burner going.' He looked at his pal sympathetically. 'He's all squished up. Come on, Elliott!'

'Come on, Elliott!' cried Lampie excitedly, grateful for the dragon's comforting presence.

'Come on, Elliott!' breathed Nora, a prayer in her voice.

The dragon knew a great deal was at stake. A ship in distress – and his own reputation. He made his maximum effort though it was difficult for a dragon to get his bellows going under such cramped conditions. He was wedged tight and very uncomfortable. Pulling faces, puffing, blowing and panting, he finally belched forth a brilliant flame. But only for an instant. A heavy gust of wind and rain doused his valiant effort.

'Again, Elliott, again,' Pete clenched his hands tight. The dragon just had to succeed. No-one else could light the wick.

Elliott felt a surge of confidence. He told himself he could do it . . . and he did! The next belch of dazzling flame caused the wicks to flare. Seconds later, the life-saving beam shone again across the churning waters. The lighthouse was operational.

Only just in time . . .

The distressed vessel was struggling in the storm. In the stygian gloom nothing was visible as Paul and the helmsman struggled frantically with the wheel, sweat mingling on their foreheads with the spray. They had no illusions. In such a storm their chances of survival were slim, without the lighthouse beam to guide them. The decks were awash and the men slipped and slithered in an effort to keep their feet.

Suddenly, incredibly, a long finger of light swept the murky sea. It was a miracle.

'Look there,' cried the man at the wheel.

'It's the Passamaquoddy Light,' yelled Paul. 'That means the rocks are dead ahead!' It was a moment of crisis.

'Hard right rudder,' ordered the captain.

The ship had been headed straight for the cruel rocks waiting to devour them. Now, with luck, they might swing clear.

Lampie, Nora, Pete and his dragon watched the drama below. When they saw the ship steer away from the rocks they cheered.

Pete hugged Elliott. 'Elliott! Elliott! Oh . . . you did it!'

Lampie stared out across the churning foam, a faraway look in his eyes, a dreamy quality in his voice. 'He saved the ship, that's what he did!'

Nora's eyes sparkled with excitement. 'Elliott's so wonderful. I could give him a big kiss!'

Elliott suddenly beamed as brightly as the beacon he had just lit.

Pete giggled. 'He'd love it!'

Nora held her head to one side and murmured, 'All right, I will!' She approached the dragon, smiling happily.

Elliott was overcome with shyness. He blushed to the roots of his pink hair, turning all colours. Even his green coat changed to purple. He wriggled . . . he squirmed . . . and was ready to burst. It was all too much. Bashful and retiring . . . he did in fact retire. He made himself invisible!

Nora arched her fine brows in surprise. Then she laughed. Dear, lovable, unpredictable Elliott!

The storm blew itself out during the night and by morning the wild wind had dropped to a whisper. Finally it lay down with a lingering sigh. The sea, incredibly blue beneath an azure sky, jetted gently around the jutting rocks. The mingling essence of pine and seaweed wafted on the warm, capricious air. Dawn's first flush illuminated the hills and the village had a newly laundered look.

Pete, Nora and Lampie slept little through the previous night but Nora and her father were up very early. When Pete awoke he leapt from his bunk, poured himself a cup of coffee, then dashed upstairs to join the others. Lampie was clearing up the storm's debris and Nora was polishing the lens, humming as she worked.

Pete ran straight to the window and stared out. 'Look! All the fishing boats!' he cried excitedly pointing towards the harbour.

Lampie straightened up and looked through the telescope. 'Let's see what's going on down there,' he said.

Nora dropped her duster and without pause she hurried with Pete and Lampie from the lighthouse, heading towards the wharf. In the morning light, the white, blue, pink and yellow houses had a neat, trim appearance. The air vibrated with a sense of jubilation. Children danced on the village green.

At the wharf, the fisherman laughed and joked as they brought their catch ashore. Such a catch it was, they had not seen so many

117

fish in many years. The villagers were gathered round, watching events and waiting to thank the brave dragon who had saved a ship from certain disaster, and brought a harvest of fish to their shores.

While they waited, they sang:

'A dragon, a dragon,
You bet we saw a dragon.
So big and brave he came to save
A village in distress.
He kept the ship from crashing
When he heard the S.O.S.
He faced a group of villains
And he fought them with success!

He's great, he's great,
A chum, a pal, a mate!
A dragon, a dragon,
We're proud to love a dragon.
Before he came to fight the storm,
The night was dark and dim.
Now every roof and window is
Repaired because of him!

He filled the ocean up with fish,
He packed it to the brim.
We want it known
That he's our very own!'

The village children stopped playing on the swings and see-saw to chant:

'There's room for everyone in this world
If everyone makes some room.
Won't you move over and share this world?
Everyone make some room!'

Nora, Lampie and Pete moved among the villagers. Even Miss Taylor stopped ringing the school bell and hastened to join the revellers. She even joined Nora in praising the valiant dragon:

'Even a dragon deserves a place,
A wide open space, with no reigns, no chains.
He wants to play games, to dance with you.
Give him a chance to sing his song.
He only wants to belong!

From an ant to a bird to an elephant herd
Let them walk, and fly, and roam.
Step aside, let them live, it's simple to give
Like us, they just need a home.

There's room for everyone in this world.
Will everyone make some room!
Love given freely can spare this world,
Let friendly feelings bloom!

Just give an inch, give a yard, never flinch,
When the time comes to offer a hand.
Let's make sure
We give everyone somewhere to stand.
Just the way God planned it,
Just the way God planned!'

A shout carried above the noise of the crowd, a voice strangely
familiar.

'Nora! Nora!' Like an echo from the past!

For a moment, Nora could not move. A tremor passed through
her body, her hands felt like ice. Slowly, she forced herself to turn
round. Sheer shock drained every vestige of colour from her face.
She was looking at Paul. Paul, in seaman's clothing, a duffle bag
slung over his shoulder, his arms outstretched in welcome.

'Nora!' he cried again.

'Paul!' With a choking sensation in her throat she ran blindly
towards him. For a tiny fraction of time they held each other at
arm's length eagerly searching each other's faces. Then she was
close in Paul's arms, the innermost secret of her heart expressed in
her tawny eyes. They hugged, kissed, wept . . . spoke muffled
words.

The stillness, the deep sense of loneliness which Nora had felt
for so long all disappeared in a moment.

Behind them Lampie was shouting in a voice filled with laughter
and incredulity. 'Paul's come back! Paul's back!'

'What happened to you?' Nora had at least a hundred questions
to ask the tall, handsome man at her side.

Paul slipped his arm about her slender waist. 'My ship collided
with another in a storm off Cape Hatteras. I was the only survivor.'
He looked grave, recalling the fate of his shipmates on that last
fateful voyage. 'When I woke up in the hospital, I'd lost my
memory.'

'Yes . . . go on . . .' prompted Nora eagerly.

Paul hesitated. He looked mystified. 'Then, the other day a

strange thing happened! My bed tipped over, I don't how, I bumped my head . . . and suddenly, everything came back to me!'

'It's a miracle!' boomed the Mayor who had joined the villagers on the wharf.

'It's Elliott!' insisted Pete in a loud voice.

Lampie clapped his hands. 'That's right! Pete said Elliott had found Paul.'

Paul was definitely confused. 'Elliott? Pete?' he asked.

Nora put her arms on Pete's shoulders and smiled down at him with affection in her eyes. 'This is Pete,' she said to Paul, introducing them to each other. 'He lives with us.'

Pete and Paul shook hands, immediately liking each other.

'Hi, Paul.'

'Hi, Pete.'

Pete asked the sailor, 'Would you please thank Elliott? He likes to be appreciated.'

Paul's eyes crinkled humorously. 'Okay, sure, I'll thank him. Where is he?'

'Right here.'

Paul stared all round. 'I don't see . . .'

Nora could not repress a mischievous giggle. 'Just say, "thank you, Elliott," to that space right there.'

'What?' Paul, nonplussed, wondered if everyone was crazy. Elliott grinned invisibly. Nora sang:

> 'He has the head of a camel,
> The neck of a crocodile;
> It sounds rather strange.
> He's both a fish and a mammal,
> And I hope he'll never change!
> 'Cause it's not easy
> To find someone who cares.
> I'm glad we found him, we love him,
> We won't let him get away,
> 'Cause it's not easy . . .'

Paul frowned.

> 'You say the head of a camel,
> The neck of a crocodile?'

Pete and Lampie yelled enthusiastically:

> 'And the ears of a *cow*!'

*

Paul, half-accepting these odd facts, answered:

> 'It's clear that friends can be different.
> Yes, I understand that now!'

Nora and Paul joined in the next chorus:

> 'It's so easy
> To share somebody's dream.
> It gets easy
> When you work as a team!'

Pete laughed:

> 'You've got to tend it, fan it!'

Paul cuddled Nora:

> 'That's what I plan to do.
> I had one friend on my side.
> Now I have two –
> Her and you!'

Paul pulled Pete over beside him ruffling his hair.

'And Elliott!' reminded Pete.

'Oh, yes,' thought Paul. I must thank Elliott.' Feeling rather foolish he spoke to the space where he was assured Elliott was waiting. 'Well, I just want to say thank you, Elliott, sir, for everything.' Paul stepped back and turned to ask Pete, 'That okay?'

Pete nodded. 'He liked that a lot. Especially when you called him "sir".'

The Mayor, pompous, filled with a sense of his own importance on this special morning in the village of Passamaquoddy, had decided it was time for a speech. Holding up his hands for silence, he addressed the crowds.

'Ladies, gentlemen, children . . .'

'And dragon,' interrupted Pete.

'And dragon,' echoed the Mayor dutifully. He leaned towards Pete. 'There's just one, right?'

'Right!'

The Mayor coughed, then continued. 'Yes, and especially the dragon. What a wonderful and joyous occasion this is.' He beamed all round. 'And it's wonderful and joyous only because of one person . . . well, he isn't exactly a person . . . and he isn't exactly an animal.' He paused. 'I don't know what he is, exactly!'

'A dragon,' muttered Pete, simplifying the issue.

The Mayor squared his shoulders and agreed. 'That's exactly what he is. And Pete, the Council would like to thank Elliott the dragon on behalf of the township.'

'He's standing right there,' said Pete, indicating a space. 'He'd appreciate it if you'd thank him yourself.'

The Mayor squinted in the strong sunlight. 'You mean . . . I can actually . . . talk right to him?'

'Of course!'

'Go right to the source, I always say,' murmured the Mayor.

'Elliott, on behalf . . .' He moved forward towards the dragon, and unable to see him, ran smack into Elliott flattening his cigar on the invisible bulk. He backed away looking nervous, trying to recover his dignity.

'Right . . . er . . . yes, well, Elliott? Just want to . . . er . . . say thanks on behalf of the township of Passaqua . . . Quassapamod . . .' In vain he sought to recall the name of his own township.

The demoralising moment was glossed over by a clanking sound approaching the wharf. Everyone turned to stare. Doc Terminus and Hoagy, crumpled and dishevelled, were on their wagon. How they had escaped from the jail was anybody's guess . . . but there they were.

Despite his recent skulduggery, the doctor was still optimistic, hoping he could con the villagers and make himself a fortune. Bold as brass he stood up as the wagon drew level with the crowd, raised his battered hat and sang:

> 'Will everybody listen!
> I can build a circus here.
> Elliott the dragon –
> See his name in lights!
> I'll feed and maintain him,
> Rehearse him and train him.
> He'll walk on wire, jump through fire,
> Bring in every ticket buyer!'

The locals screamed indignantly:

> 'You keep your hands off Elliott!'

Doc Terminus was not one to give up easily:

> 'Folks will pay to see

The only dragon anywhere.
We'll be getting richer by the day.'

Yelled the townsfolk:

'Go away!'

Terminus persisted:

'Hear them acclaim us,
This town will be famous,
The whole wide world will look at us and say:
Pa-do-ma-quas-sy . . .
Pa-qua-ma-sod-dy . . .
Pas-sa-ma-mas-sy . . .
Quo-da-ma-pod-dy . . .
Pas-sa-ma-dad-dy . . .
Quo-da-ma-pas-sy . . .'

In ringing tones, every throat uttered,

'Pas-sa-ma-quod-dy!'

The locals had seen – and heard more than enough of the villainous doctor. The Mayor and Councillors moved forward in a body and the doctor's interpretation was correct. It was time to move . . . but fast!

As their wagon disappeared round a bend the villagers' cries rang in their ears. '*Passamaquoddy!*'

Paul and Nora laughed, then Nora whispered in Paul's ear, 'I still make the best clam chowder on the Main coast.'

He kissed her and whispered a reply, and they headed back in the direction of the lighthouse.

The crowd at the wharf thinned. Housewives purchased fish from the stalls, and the children were summoned into school. Pete trailed some distance behind Paul, Nora and Lampie. He wanted to be alone with Elliott.

Pete and his dear dragon wandered up the hillside towards the orchard where they had munched apples on that first morning before they had actually entered the village. So much had happened in a few short days. Pete flung himself down on the grass and motioned to his friend to sit beside him.

He stared into the dragon's face in admiration. 'Elliott, you're the greatest. You've made so many people happy. I'm proud of you.'

Elliott grunted and made a soft, musical, yet sad sound which Pete clearly understood.

Pete's face turned bright pink. 'What do you mean . . . you have to go?'

Elliott replied.

'Someone else needs you?' Pete looked downcast. 'You'll come back, won't you?' he asked anxiously.

Elliott's reply to that question caused tears to prick Pete's eyelids. 'Do you mean I won't ever see you again . . . ever?'

Elliott sounded regretful.

Pete sobbed. 'But I don't know whether I can live without you!'

Elliott whispered.

'I'm not being silly,' insisted Pete, rubbing his eyes. 'Wait! Don't go yet!'

Elliott told his friend in dragon language that he had to go. Other duties called.

'Please . . . can I see you . . . for the last time?' pleaded Pete, trying not to cry again.

Elliott emerged by degrees. 'More . . . more . . .' cried Pete. 'Come on – the whole thing!'

The dragon appeared in his full splendour, from wing-tip, to tail, to lovable face and pink hair.

'Ah, you look wonderful,' breathed Pete, a break in his voice. He flung his arms round the dragon, murmuring tearfully, 'I'll never forget you.' The dragon sat down and Pete pressed his cheek against Elliott's cheek, kissing him. 'I love you, Elliott.' Their tears mingled. The dragon was crying, too.

Elliott sniffed loudly and stood up. Pete ran to his side. 'Now remember to listen to whoever you go to next, and don't scare people . . . and remember – you're supposed to be invisible!'

Pete had a big lump in his throat. It was hard to say goodbye – very hard – but a dragon had his responsibilities, too. Somewhere else in the world another boy . . . or a girl . . . would require his help.

Fighting back more tears, Pete cried, 'Goodbye, Elliott,' as the dragon rose into the blue sky, higher and higher away.

Pete raced down the hill and along the beach, waving as he ran. He caught up with Nora, Lampie and Paul who were all waiting, sensing that they would soon be losing Elliott. They all looked skywards and waved together. Nora had no doubts that Elliott was on the side of the angels. He had brought back her own true love. She squeezed Paul's hand.

From high above them, Elliott flipped his wings and blew a final kiss. Pete blinked bravely and Nora held out her arms to the red-haired, freckle-faced, brave little boy. He ran to her and his hand

rested warm and snug in her clasp. He knew that he had found true friendship, and with it, the greatest gift of all.

The gift of love!